BEWARE THE MINDS YOU ENTER

7 Horror Stories to Keep You Up At Night

Written by JP Charles

CONTENTS

STORY ONE

THE SHOES WE WEAR

Fatigue had encumbered Sonia for the duration of the long drive to her new lake house from the airport. She could feel a sense of relief as the long driveway came into view, presented silently in the light of her high-beams. The subtle feeling of relief gradually blossomed into a strong sense of accomplishment. Sonia was finally acknowledging herself for being able to complete the last minute job that called her away from her family so suddenly, and she got it done earlier than expected. She smiled with a sense of satisfaction as she recited the spiritual affirmation she had recited to herself anytime she faced a complicated task.

"I can do all things through Christ who strengthens me."

She did believe the verse and leaned on it for confidence throughout her life. This time, the reward for her hard efforts and sacrifice was a relaxing four day weekend at her new lake house. She felt truly blessed for finding this house at such a low price in a small mountain town that seemed like it had been separated from the stresses of the modern world for decades. A calm peace filled her as she approached her hide away home, her headlights creating a glimmer off the surface of the placid water just behind her winding driveway. She paused for a moment before pulling into the small garage that was adjoined to the house. She just wanted a moment to take in the view. Even at midnight, it was a breathtaking sight. The silhouette of the mountains just beyond the lake, highlighted by a brightly lit moon and bright stars. Sonia had never seen so many stars in her life. And to top it off, the lake reflected the exact image of mountains and night sky brilliantly. She had never seen anything like it. With a huge and pleasant smile on her face, Sonia looked to her neighbor's home, several hundred yards down to her right. Her house was the last on the road, and one of only ten in the entire development. She could see only one light on in the window of her neighbor's home, but as soon as she noticed it, it suddenly went out.

"I wonder if they ever get tired of the view?" she said aloud. "I'll introduce myself tomorrow morning after breakfast, or even better, after brunch."

Sonia headed into the house after parking her car in the garage, right next to the blue four door that was already parked and resting silently. She moaned with sweet relieve as she took off her designer shoes and dropped them at the door. She looked up from her feet and toward the living room, then sharply gasped in shock as she laid eyes on the biggest mess she had ever walked into. Everything had been toppled, turned over and scattered all over the room. Furniture, drawers, clothes, and even books, scattered all across the living room floor! Strangely, none of the framed pictures on the wall were touched, nor the vases damaged. Her initial reaction was fear, but she began to consider who she left in charge while she was away. Immediately, she rolled her eyes and groaned loudly with frustration.

"What the hell, Ramsey" she exclaimed as she walked gingerly through the mess. Sonia felt her anger growing inside her. "You guys went way overboard this time! I can't even walk into my new lake house for the first time without putting up with your stupid jokes, seriously!" She then let out a sudden yelp as she stepped her stocking covered foot down into a liquid puddle on the floor. "You are too old for this crap, it's not funny anymore", she shouted angrily. "And what kind of example are you trying to make for Sophia!?"

Sonia's brother, Ramsey, thought he was a riot. Although very intelligent and a hard worker, he had been the class clown his entire life, to the point of not knowing when to quit. Even funerals were not exempt from his often poorly timed pranks. And every single one of his pranks was always at the expense of an unsuspecting victim. To make matters worse over this particular trip, he was paired up with his lifelong friend, Tyler. Although usually reserved, Tyler was actually Sonia's best friend since childhood, he could not resist making himself an accessory to every one of Ramsey's pranks. Sonia always figured participating as Ramsey's partner in crime was secretly Tyler's method of avoiding being at the expense of Ramsey's pranks himself. Despite all this, she knew the two were reliable and had proven themselves time and time again as dependable guardians for her six year old daughter, whom they were taking care of while Sonia was away for business.

Sonia walked on her tip toes, circling what appeared to be puddles of water that glistened across the floor.

"Sweet lord, you people can sure make a mess!" She dropped her bags on the floor and picked up her phone from her purse. Stretching her back and yawning loudly, Sonia debated whether or not she should have them clean up the mess now, or in the morning. She figured since neither Ramsey nor Tyler responded to her remarks, they were either asleep or waiting somewhere in the house to jump out and scare her. But considering it was passed midnight and she did not tell either of them she would be arriving a day early, they were most likely sleeping. It had been a long drive, and she was ready to just drop down somewhere and sleep it off. The earful they were set to receive would just have to wait until the morning, or even better, after breakfast. She had worked very hard, and she deserved eight solid hours of sleep.

Walking wearily to the hallway that led to her bedroom, she took one final look over her shoulder at the mess before heading to bed for the night. "I've been away for like two seconds and they have turned my house upside down, this is outrageous!" she mumbled to herself as she headed down the hallway. Skipping over clothes that were scattered across the floor, Sonia carefully made her way to her room. A sudden loud clatter froze her in her tracks. Realizing the noise came from behind her, Sonia slowly turn around, ready to unleash her anger on whoever came out of that direction.

"Ramsey! Ramsey!!" she called out expecting to see her brother and best friend jump out in an attempt to get a scream out of her.

"Ramsey, is that you? Where is Sophia?" she asked as she walked down and towards the place where the noise had come from.

The room remained quiet and her voice clearly echoed, in which she could actually detect a bit of fear. An uncomfortable, eerie feeling began to settle over her as she searched for an explanation within her mind as to what could have caused that sudden noise. She looked around the house and realized the door she had walked in from, and had closed and locked behind her, was now open. Gripped by fear, Sonia began to realize the disorganization in the room was very random, but limited to only the living room. She began to get the impression the mess was not the result of a prank, but a desperate struggle. Her eyes dropped to the puddle on the floor she had stepped in. Reaching down with her hand, she grasped her stocking firmly and then brought her fingers to her nose. Taking a few scared whiffs, when recognized the odor coming from her fingers to be not that of water, but urine. Her eyes widened and her breath cut sharply as she realized she was standing in the middle of a crime scene. Her heart slammed in her chest. She looked around quickly with her eyes, her body still frozen with fear. Sonia's mind raced as she played possible scenarios in her head as what might have happened to her loved ones. She closed her eyes and took the thoughts out from her mind. She suddenly remembered parking next to Ramsey's rental car in the garage, and seeing his shoes by the door, right where she dropped hers.

"Is he still here in the house, did he call the police, are they all at the police station?" her mind continued to race with her heartbeat.

Then just as sudden as the thought came to her, Sonia dashed to the master bedroom door. Panic filled her as she raced to where her daughter most like would have been sleeping until she arrived. Greeted by a strong, putrid smell as she reached the door, she slowly grasped the knob with her shaking hand, almost terrified of what she may find on the other side. Her heart was beating with such force she could feel her own pulse thundering from her hand into the doorknob. The smell was even stronger now, and unlike anything she had ever experienced. It was so thick, she could virtually taste it.

"This is my house; I will not be afraid of anything!" Sonia firmly whispered to herself as she slowly turned the knob. In one solid thrust, she pushed the door all the way open. In an instant, she took in the most horrifying sight she had ever witnessed. Standing there frozen for a moment with her eyes and mouth wide open, Sonia's already quaking knees finally gave out from under her. She collapsed in the doorway, trembling from head to toe. The cold sweat from her face was washed away by the warm tears streaming down her face. She opened her mouth to scream, but the sounds would not come out. All she could do was stare into the gruesome sight like a person lost in thought.

In front of her laying on her bed, were the decomposing remains of three badly dismembered bodies. The heads and limbs had been removed leaving only the torsos, which appeared to be riddled with lacerations. To add to the carnage, there were several birds picking at the torso closest to Sonia. It was apparent they have flown in through the open window at the other end of the room. The three bodies lay side by side as if they were placed in order. One torso was without clothing, and it appeared the victim was male. However, if that was the case, he had been castrated. The other two were clothed, one wearing a designer shirt she recognized to belong to her brother, Ramsey. The buttons were missing and the shirt wide open revealing a Celtic cross, the very one Ramsey got for his 18th birthday. Sonia's heart sank and she was filled with grief. She tried to scream and cry but still could not force any sound from her mouth. Sonia had begun to feel faint and the room suddenly began to spin. She suddenly felt sick to her stomach and could not control the heavy flow of vomit that escaped her body. Heave after heave, Sonia through up for what seemed like an eternity. Even still, her mind raced, but her thoughts were too mixed up for even her to grasp.

Sonia forced herself to look up again at the grotesque scene, specifically toward the remains of the third torso, farthest away from her. She began to realize something about that torso wasn't quite right. She crawled to the corner of the bed to get a better look. Her eyes widened when she realized it was the torso of an adult women. "Not Sophia", she stammered as her heart sharply skipped a beat. "That's not Sophia. That's not Sophia!"

Forcing herself back to feet, Sonia's mind was consumed by the realization that her daughter was not one of the three bodies on the bed. Her mind spun wildly as her eyes darted around the room, searching for a sign of her. Sophia was nowhere to be seen. For a brief moment, a slight feeling of hope began to arise from the chaos that consumed Sonia's being. She took a single forward step toward the doorway when she stepped on something she was very familiar with, as she had stepped on it a hundred times before. It was Sophia's favorite doll. A small blond girl with pigtails in a plaid school dress. Sophia clung to this everywhere she went whenever separated from her mother. Sonia's instinct was to reach for it, but she realized the doll was in the middle of some kind of stain. A dark brown stain leading from the bed to the closed bathroom door. Sonia's heart sank again once she realized the stain was a trail of dried blood, and that she was likely to find her daughter just beyond on the other side of the door.

She blankly stared at the door through the tears that were starting to form at the corners of her eyes. In her mind, she uncontrollably played out scenes of what condition she'd find her daughter in. She stared blankly, unable to move, unable to blink.

The sound of a hollow thud coming from what sounded like the bathtub quickly brought life to her body. Before she could even give a second thought, she raced to the bathroom door and swung it wide open.

She stood in the doorway, frozen for a brief moment. The bathroom was intact; the walls retained their sparkly white color and the only thing that could suggest even the remotest violence was the thin trail of blood leading to the bath tub, and a few spots of blood on the edge of the closed shower curtain. Sonia gasped as she looked down to see a little girl up to her neck in red water staring blankly back up at her. Her already fair skin was nearly white as snow, and her lips were virtually blue. Sonia held her breath, looking for some sign of life in her daughter. "Mom-my", a faint whisper emerged from the child's pasty lips.

"Sophia!!!" Sonia shouted, finally managing to get full sound from her mouth. "Oh my God, Sophia!"

Sonia grabbed her daughter from the tub and cradled her in her arms, crying. She examined her from head to toe, wiping away the diluted blood, searching for any kind of injuries. From what she could tell, Sophia had not been physically harmed. She could feel the six year old quivering all over. Sonia knew this was a good sign that her tiny body was fighting to keep itself alive. Sonia began to cry uncontrollably as she imagined her little girl hiding in the tub for days, too afraid to move from it. Too afraid to go for help. "Help", Sonia muttered. "I'm going to get us help baby!" she exclaimed loudly into her daughter's ear.

Sonia ran with her daughter into the living room to retrieve her phone from her purse, all the while repeating, "Oh, my God... Oh my God..." almost uncontrollably. Sonia was fighting a type of anxiety she had never experienced in her life. Even she could not fathom exactly how distressed she was. Grabbing her purse off the floor with one hand and holding her daughter with the other, Sonia ran into the kitchen. She laid her daughter on the breakfast bar, still bundled in the towel. Her mind raced as she scrambled through her purse for the phone. "How could this possibly have happened? Who did this? Why on earth did she bring her daughter to a place that was brand new to even her?" All these questions without answers raced through her mind as she opened her phone to call 911.

Two Weeks Earlier

"Mommy... Mommy..." Sonia looked around at the usually bubbly six year old behind her. She was putting her bag in her car in preparation for work travel that she had been called for halfway into their vacation. The girl, now standing in the front doorway, had been sulking all day, and Sonia knew exactly why. She couldn't possibly be upset with her. Sonia's work gave her little time to spend with her daughter, and it was as frustrating for her as much as it was hurtful for Sophia.

"Hmmm?" She took her time to answer to imply how little desire she had to have this conversation again.

"Mommy, can you try to make it back sooner?" Sophie asked. Approaching the door, Sonia came face to face with the large, beautiful blue eyes that were pleading directly with her own heart. Sonia's heart broke every time this happened, and it happened often.

"I'll try..." she said after swallowing hard.

"Promise me mommy, promise me you'll be back soon... Pinky promise!" Sonia knew not to make any promises she could not keep. But she was also looking into Sophie's watery blue eyes and there was no resisting that. She stooped lower and used her hands as support by placing them on her knees.

"Soph, I can't promise that I'll be home earlier than expected", she hesitated, "but I can promise I'll get you a lot of beautiful things on my way back home." The girl jerked out of her way as if she had been stung by a bee.

"I don't want anything!" she exclaimed in bold defiance. "You buy me things all the time, but I don't want them." She then promptly stormed away into the house.

"Sophie I need to work" Sonia exclaimed as she pursued her daughter into the house. "I have to work! If I don't work, we will starve!" she scolded.

The girl suddenly stopped walking and turned angrily to face her mother, wearing her frustration and pain all over her face... "Then let us starve, I want my mother!" Sophia then ran down the hallway toward her room.

Sonia stood there, feeling almost dumbfounded. Sophia was right; she needed a mother. More than anything else, she needed a mother. Sonia's heart was crushed, and for a moment, she considered canceling her trip and staying with her baby instead. She considered quitting the job altogether for the sake of her daughter. But the reality of living paycheck to paycheck suddenly hit her, and quickly reminded herself why she worked so hard to get the position she was now in to begin with. Sonia took a deep breath, went to her daughter's room to see her sulking silently on the bed. Slowly taking a seat next to her, Sonia took another deep breath as she searched for the right thing to say to her little girl. "Well..." was all Sonia cold get from her mouth before her daughter cut her off saying, "Just go mommy, I'll be fine."

That was the straw that broke the camel's back for Sonia. She realized with the force of a slap that her daughter had given up hope that she would actually ever have a complete relationship with her mother. Sonia's heart became heavy, and she could feel pressure building up behind her eyes as if she were about to cry. Sonia didn't want her daughter to be "fine" without her. She wanted to be there, all the way, all the time. She knew she had to stop compromising her daughter, and start compromising for her. She swallowed hard and looked at the girl. She was more matured than the average six-year-old and she knew that no cock and bull story would suffice in this case. She needed something concrete. She turned to Sophia abruptly and said:

"Sophie, how about we do this; why don't you go with your uncles Ramsey and Tyler to the lake house we just got, and I'll meet you guys there as soon as I get back. I promise you, I'll do everything I can to finish this work trip early so I can meet you there and we can spend the rest of the week together. On top of that, you and I will stay there until school resumes, just the two of us!" It was like magic, the girl's eyes brightened up so fast that is seemed like someone had switched on a light bulb in a pitch black room. A beautiful babyish smile filled her face up and Sophia wrapped her little arms around her mother's neck, giving her a huge kiss on the cheek. "Yayyyyy, I'm so happy mommy!" Sophia exclaimed through her jubilation.

The girl suddenly leapt out of the embrace and grabbed her mother's hand shouting, "You're going to miss your flight if we don't hurry! Come on now!" Sonia laughed with a renewed energy as her daughter pulled her by the hand to the car, where Ramsey was waiting with the engine running. He eagerly embraced Sophia and picked her up as Sonia got into the driver's seat.

As Sonia drove away, she looked into the rear view mirror for one more glimpse at Ramsey and Sophia smiling and waving goodbye. Once they were out of sight, she had leaned back in the chair and smiled. Her mind was made up; she would do whatever needed to be done to keep the promise she had made to the most important person in the world.

Sonia suddenly snapped back to reality once she realized the poor girl shaking in her arms had started to shake even more. "You're going to be okay baby," she said wondering if Sophia was even grasping her words. Sonia sat on the only seat in the kitchen, cradling her little girl in her arms trying to warm her body. Sophia seemed to be drifting in and out of consciousness and Sonia looked at her helplessly as she waited for the ambulance and police to arrive. It had been fifteen minutes since she had called 911. It wasn't until she made the call that she realized how far the lake house was from town. As she sat there, she refused to let herself think of what had happened to the people in her house. She wasn't ready to think about it; she would wait till her baby was fine before she let herself grieve for the people she was certain met their fate in the house.

Her face was flush with tears and all she could do was hold her child in her arms. She held her close but she wondered if there wasn't something more she could do until the paramedics arrived. She remembered seeing the neighbor's lights go out just before she came inside the house. That was less than half an hour ago, maybe they were still awake or just lightly sleeping.

The 911 operator had instructed her to keep the girl in one spot till they arrived and not to move her until she has been stabilized. But what if her neighbors could somehow help Sophia in the meantime.

And what if the monster that had done this to her family came back while they were waiting. The very thought of that nearly put her into a panic. Just then she thought, "But what if the neighbors had something to do with this? I'd be walking my baby into a trap. If I can first determine they are safe, I can bring them here to her. But that means I would have to leave her." So many scenarios filled her head, but she knew for certain and above all else that time was fleeting by the second and the more time went by, the less the likelihood that her baby would survive either way. She had to make her decision and follow through, now!

Torn between staying at her baby's side and going to look for help, she decided to hide Sophia in the back seat of her car in the garage. Sonia had the only set of keys to the car, so only she would be able to get her hands on her. After reassuring the barely conscious child she would return for her quickly, Sonia shut of the garage light and exited through the main door.

She had barely made it halfway across the front lawn when she saw the light in the neighbor's house was once again lit. She nearly shouted with excitement as she broke into a full sprint toward the house. Although Sonia was very athletic, reality hit her that the house was several hundred yards away. However, Sophia's life was depending on her, and Sonia quickly made up her mind that she would run the entire distance as fast as she could, for the sake of her daughter. Sonia knew she was running faster than she ever had in her life, but it still seemed like it took an eternity for her to reach their driveway. Exhausted and breathing erratically, Sonia finally reached the porch and shuffled up the few low steps to the door. She loosely raised her shaking hand to knock on the door, but heard a shriek come from the inside of the house just before she knocked.

"What the hell was that?" Sonia asked herself, fear once again taking control of her. She hesitated, half expecting to hear another shriek come from inside the house. Moments passed, but not a sound arose. Sonia began to wonder if perhaps all the anxiety and stress of this situation was causing her mind to play tricks on her. Perhaps it was just in her head, and she was hearing things.

Just as soon as she allowed herself to be convinced that this was indeed the case, the sound of shattering glass quickly interrupted that short instance of peaceful quiet. She could then hear the footsteps crushing the glass and fade away toward the rear of the house. She put her hand down, realizing that the killer who had been to her house might be the one inside this house right now. Sonia decided to call 911 again, but just realized she locked the phone in the car with her daughter.

A moment passed as Sonia wondered what she should do. If there was a chance the people inside the house were still alive, they would surely be killed and mutilated by the time the cops arrived. But if she decided to go in unprepared and attempt to help them, the killer would likely do the same to her. Sonia decided the only logic choice was to return to her daughter, lock the garage, and call the police again to let them know the killer was just one house away, and the people there were most likely badly injured or already dead.

Sonia turned away from the door and began walking away slowly, as not to make any noise to alert the killer to her presence.

"If you take one more step, I will blow your head off!" a man's voice said from the shadows masking the side of the garage.

Sonia froze in her tracks, just steps away from the driveway. She thought to herself, "What do I do now?" She could hear the man's footsteps stepping lightly over the gravel, approaching her quickly from behind. Her heart raced as she scrambled in her mind for the next step. Suddenly she saw a white flash and felt herself falling forward. Just before everything went black, Sonia looked to her left and saw a pair of black shoes just inches from her face.

As Sonia finally began to slowly come to, she realized she was in a home. She was laying on something soft, perhaps a mattress. As she began to look around to get some sort of idea of what was going on, she felt a sharp pain shoot through her neck and up to the top of her head. As she winced from the pain, her sense of smell quickly overtook her mind. There was a smell in the room, a thick smell that nearly made her gag. A smell very similar to the once of decaying flesh back in her own bedroom. She wanted to pinch her nose closed to rid herself of the putrid odor, but realized she could not because her hands were bound behind her back. In that instance, she realized the peril of her situation.

"Oh, my God! He's got me... He's got me..." she thought to herself.

"You're awake, "a low and disturbingly calm voice rose from the surrounding darkness. She stiffened at the sound of the voice, remaining still and not knowing if she should say anything.

"Do you know why you're here?" the man asked.

Sonia rolled her eyes around the dark room, searching for her captor and tormentor. "Nnnnhhhh", that was all she could manage to see as just then, she realized even her mouth was bound. At this moment, her emotions went from fear to anger and defiance. It was a good thing her attacker put a gag in her mouth, otherwise her response would have been along the lines of, "Because you're a bloodthirsty sociopath that derives pleasure in other people's pain!" But Sonia knew she dared not provoke him. If there was even the tiniest chance that she could get to see her baby again, it would not be because she decided to antagonize a killer.

"Please let me go," she mumbled through the fabric that impaired her speech. She could feel her captor's hands untie the knot that bound the gag tightly into her mouth.

"What was that?" he teased.

"I haven't seen your face, I don't know who you are, and I have never heard your voice before", Sonia pleaded in the hopes that he would find reason in her words. The response she got was a resounding laughter that filled the room with its richness. Sonia tensed up; the smell from the other side of the room was strong again. She began choking from the smell and knew it had to be decomposing flesh, just like back at her lake house.

This severed head was much withered and the skin was various shades of brown and dark green. The eyes were wide open and nearly all white. There, lying just behind the head, was the body of a middle aged women, covered in blood. This must have been the person who shrieked as Sonia approached the house. The woman was clearly dead, but blood still poured from her many gaping wounds. It appeared as though the killer had taken an axe to her head, striking her several times in the face.

With her eyes filled with tears resulting from a mixture of fear and the horrible smell, she pleaded "This place stinks so badly. Please, do you mind putting me somewhere else?" A deafening silence fell over the room. She pondered if she should repeat her request just as she heard a frustrated grunt escape the man that was holding her captive.

He raised himself from the bed, flipping her over and she immediately made eye contact with the source of the foul smell. It was the severed, rotting head of an adult woman. Sonia began dry heaving immediately as she choked on the thick stench filling her nostrils. It was obvious whoever this belonged to, it was not to any of the people who were killed in this house or hers.

Sonia's captor suddenly picked up the severed head by the crust that was its hair and looked into its eyes, shaking it angrily shouting, "This is your entire fault Miss B, you mess the place up with your stink, now we have a guest that hasn't been here one day and she's already offended! I hate it when you do this! I hate it! I hate it!" Realizing the man was sick with madness, Sonia dared not look up into his face. Although terrified, she was determined to give him any more resolve to kill her than he had already given himself. Sonia thought to herself, "This guy is bat shit crazy, and he gets off on this shit! There is no way he is going to let me go." She realized her only chance of survival was escape. She just needed to find a way.

The man threw the rotting head back onto the bed and stormed out through the door. The very second he was gone, Sonia started to squirm in effort to free her hands of the bindings. She wiggled and strained against the ropes, trying to create even the slightest bit of space, but her efforts ultimately accomplished nothing. Seeing that there was no way she could get out of the ropes, she began sobbing. Her mind raced to her daughter. Not knowing her condition and imagining her dying in the car alone caused Sonia to burst into tears.

"How much stupider can a woman be? She begged me not to leave her, she begged me... now I ..." the door opened as the killer returned to the room. She stopped crying and pretended to be asleep.

He didn't seem to notice as she spoke to her sternly in a voice that seemed as though he were annoyed or offended.

"Look, I am going to take you away from filthy old Miss B. She has always been the dirty one." He then went on mumbling about how he hated dirty people, and how he admired Sonia's choice in designer brand clothing. He complimented her on her makeup and said he got the impression that she was "of a higher class than most women." Sonia was slightly confused, but immediately hopeful that she would be able to exploit his admiration of her and be able to stall him with her charm just long enough for the police to arrive. He then stood over her and easily lifted her up, almost cradling Sonia as he had held her own daughter.

"The only thing that I hate more than dirty guests are fussy guests. Don't try anything funny or I will make you hate your life," he asserted as he carried her carefully down the hall. Sonia gently nodded in agreement and noticed a smile take his face from the corner of her eye. She had still yet to make eye contact with the man, but began to feel reassured that charming him was her one sure chance at survival. Her captor carried her passed several open windows.

The cool breeze and fresh scent of the pine trees surrounding the valley gently caressed Sonia's face.

She was certain they were still in the same house where he had knocked her out. She closed her eyes, wondering if the police had been able to locate her house and rescue her daughter. He sat her gently on the couch in the living room, facing her toward a large window which was slightly open. The big man then walked over to a nearby floor lamp and flicked the light on. Sonia was looking toward her house, hoping to get a glimpse of police pulling up into her driveway, but she could only see her own reflection off the glass, blurred by the thin white curtains that waved side to side from the light breeze.

"What is it sweetie, are you expecting a guest?" the man asked as he followed her gaze. If he had not already figured out that she had come from the house across the street, she did not want him to know. Remembering she still had the set of car keys that granted exclusive access to her daughter, she knew it would be best if she didn't give him the impression she was indeed from the next house over.

"No sir, I'm not expecting anyone. I don't even know anyone out here", she answered looking at his tie as not to be rude, but still not wanting to look at his face. The man canted his head at a slight angle as if he were a bit confused. She noticed a recliner just passed him and her black coat laid across its arm. Her keys were in it. She could only pray that he didn't go through her pockets and take it.

Sonia returned her gaze to the man standing in front of her and looked over his body quickly. Immediately, she noticed he was very well dressed.

He wore rather expensive Italian shoes, pressed slacks, button up shirt, and matching blazer all of the same designer brand. Although his attire was covered in blood spatter, she would say that his outfit alone cost him around a thousand dollars, and the value of his watch was easily double that. She could tell that the man had money, or had killed someone with a lot of money and had taken their clothing. Sonia prayed it was not the latter of the two, or else she would not have an angle to play.

"Make conversation," she pleaded with herself, "make conversation please!" She knew that in order to win him over and buy herself more time, she had to charm him, but simple compliments wouldn't do. Her words had to be sincere, or else he would see right through her.

"Is that by any means a pair of Giorgio Armani?" she warmly asked nodding at the shoes. The room was dim, and she still could not bring herself to look at his face, but she knew that finding common ground with the killer was her only chance. He looked down at his shoes as if examining them for the first time, then back up at her with a slight lean to his posture. Sonia knew she hit the mark.

"You have a very keen sense of exclusive fashion, don't you? Well, yes, they are Armani" he exclaimed with satisfaction. She forced a humble smile at the man who had just brutally killed so many people in their own homes. She didn't necessarily consider Armani to be "exclusive", but she did feel a sense of relief to know that since the man was indeed the owner of the expensive clothing he wore, her compliments would be well received.

"Well, it is a particularly nice set, must have cost a fortune." she said, aiming to inflate his ego further.

"Indeed", he said as he continued to smile. "I got this pair for four hundred, one of the less expensive pairs in my wardrobe."

Sonia's mind was working fast. She could see that he really liked to talk about himself. What questions could she ask to stall him without making it seem as though she was trying to build a profile of the man?

"Keep him talking, keep him talking," she said to herself as she smiled toward him. She knew that he was looking at her keenly now. She didn't have much time; she needed to get back to the house and get to her daughter as soon as possible.

"Four hundred? Damn that is a lot! You must be doing really well," Sonia chuckled.

"I have more money than I need... I might as well enjoy it", he replied confidently.

"You're right, life is too short," She said rather sincerely, followed by a small sob. The killer noticed her sadness and hesitated. He suddenly felt that she deserved some human treatment. After all, she had just played him a compliment in spite of her position. He turned to her and walked a little towards her. She shuddered slightly for a moment, but realized if he brought himself to her level, she would have to look into his face, which she wanted to avoid for as long as she could.

"Look, I'm going to untie you and pull up a seat so we can talk a bit. Maybe we'll find that we have more than just good fashion taste in common. But if you try anything silly, I'll make you beg for death", he warned sternly.

Seeing how he was considerate, Sonia's confidence began to rise. She might be able to pull this off and leave with her life after all. She graciously nodded at his offer to show that she understood him, and promised she would not betray his trust. To this, he smiled even more as though he had just won a game show.

As he began to untie her, Sonia kept very still and relaxed physically, but her mind raced. "I should eye gauge him and run away," she thought to herself. She immediately realized that would be foolish as the killer's muscular build was obvious even through his blazer. He was also around six feet tall. Sonia was just barely over five. If she failed to hurt him immediately with her first attempt, there would be nothing she could do to stop him from overpowering her. Taking him down wasn't an option, she'd either had to stall him until the police arrived and make a run for it, or find another opportunity to escape.

"So, if I may ask" the killer began as he sat down in a recliner just across from her, "what were you doing at the Braxton's door tonight?" As he made his enquiry, he reached into his coat and pulled out pistol, then set it gently on the wooden coffee table between them as if to show how confident he was of his dominance.

This was obviously what he hit her over the dead with after threatening to shoot her. It was short and black. Right away Sonia recognized it to be a Glock 32, the very same kind her brother had carried, concealed on his person for years.

Her heart sank once she realized that this gun was mostly taken from her brother's backpack, where he kept it hidden away from Sophia. Sonia knew there was no doubt this man had every bit of capacity necessary to kill her. She looked up into his face, desperate to find some humanity in his yes, and nearly began to plead with him about how her daughter urgently needed medical attention, but then realized he was most likely believed he had already killed Sophia, most likely in an attempt to drown her in the bath tub. She realized just then that this would only cause him to return to her house to finish the girl off.

"I got lost on my way...I was supposed to be going to Oakland. I was using the GPS on my phone, but it died and I left my charger back my house. I parked my car several houses up, which is a really far walk and have been trying to find somebody who's still awake to give me directions or let me charge my phone".

He nodded with understanding. "I've actually done that once before myself. Driving from one city to another without my charger. I drove for hours after it died, and had no idea where I was until I ended up in San Jose", he said with a chuckle. "Almost blew the entire deal I was just about to close. Well, I guess I could have let you walk away instead of bringing you inside."

Hearing this, Sonia was filled with anger, but knew it was important that she not show it. "Well, you can let me go now", she said softly. He looked at her warmly and with a slight smile, but said nothing. For the first time, Sonia took in all the details of the man's face. He had hazel color eyes with long dark lashes. His eyebrows were very dark and full, matching the color of his hair. His skin was olive, and his nose was rather pronounced. He was very handsome, and appeared as though he could be Mediterranean. Furthermore, he was obviously considerably younger than her. Despite his heavy voice and solid stature, his youthful features gave her the impression he was in his early to mid-twenties. He stood up from the seat adjusting his blazer. "I'm in the mood for some coffee, would you like some?" he asked firmly. "Yes please", she replied nodding her head in agreement.

"I am going to tie you back up now. Can't risk you running off." She knew that if he tied her up, she might lose her chance to get away. She looked at him and said with desperation coursing through every vein in her body.

"You don't need to do that. I have no idea where I am and wouldn't even know where to run. How far do you figure I could run before you get hold of me anyways? Your legs are as long as my entire body", she smirked. "It would be dumb to run. Besides, I'd rather join you in the kitchen. I could show you a special trick that makes the coffee really great."

"You're very smart, I like smart girls", he complimented with a smile. Then his face got serious.

He took her by the hand and walked toward the kitchen. All the way there, she was doing her best to act as though she hadn't realized he left the gun on the coffee table. Ramsey had taken her to the range on more than one occasion to shoot that gun. She knew that if she could somehow break away and make it to the gun first, she had a fighting chance. She could end this and finally get back to her daughter!

The anxiety began to overwhelm her. "Run now, turn and run this instant", she kept repeating in her head. His grip was relaxed, she knew she could jerk away from him. But she needed a head start. She needed to be free of his grasp in order to beat him down the long hallway.

He released her hand after entering the kitchen and playfully hoisted her onto the kitchen counter. He caressed her leg gently and complimented her on how beautiful her body is. He then gathered all the kitchen knives and tossed them under the sink, an added measure as he obviously did not trust her completely. He then plugged in the coffee maker immediately right of the sink. With his back turned, her eyes darted all over the kitchen, looking for anything that she could use to strike him over the head so she could make her run for the pistol. Seeing nothing useful, she shut her eyes angrily with frustration.

"Could you fetch me the condensed milk from the cabinet above you?" he asked as she was again struck by his politeness. "Mrs. Braxton is lactose intolerant, so she only keeps the canned stuff around." Sonia was sickened by the fact that he had brutally mutilated and murdered people he obviously had a personal relationship with. Not able to think of any diversion, she reluctantly twisted around and opened the cabinet door. Turning her neck and looking up, her eyes beheld the largest canned food item she had ever seen. As she lifted the enormous can of condensed milk, it became obvious the robust can had yet to be opened. It was full, solid, and heavy. Her pulse jumped as she realized she had just found the opportunity she was looking for, the weapon of opportunity.

Just at that moment, a distant high pitch wailing entered her ears. She looked over at her captor, who was standing frozen with her back turned to her still, looking in the direction of the sound. They both realized in the same moment that they were hearing police sirens. He spun around to face Sonia, his eyes filled with rage and his teeth bared like a wolf. Without saying a word he leapt across the kitchen toward her with such aggression that Sonia yelped loudly and dropped the large can she was holding, which landed on the counter right next to her thigh. He was on her so quickly she didn't even have time to react. Grasping her tightly by her arms as she sat stiff with her mouth wide open in shock and her eyes as large as twin moons, the killer was now face to face with her, his nose only inches away from hers.

"Please," Sonia pleaded, shaking with tears streaming from her large eyes. "I didn't call them, I've been here with you the whole time!" She knew if she wanted to make it through this, she had to win his trust. Now more so than ever, or this would be her last moment on this earth. "They must be going to a different house! There is no way they could know we are here. Let's just wait and let them go to wherever they are going, then we can leave! We can get away and won't even know we were here!" She repeated the word "we" every opportunity she had in hopes of convincing him she was in this with him. She was his, and he could trust her. "Let's just wait another minute, I promise you they aren't coming here! We can just slip out and wouldn't even know we were here!"

The man didn't say a word. He only closed his mouth and slowed his breathing. He looked deeply into her eyes, as if considering the logic in what she was saying. Sonia knew exactly where the police were heading, and although she didn't know for certain how many houses he had entered, she was aware the killer knew there was a chance the cops could be heading to one further down. She just had to convince him to wait it out and see. His eyes darted toward the sound of the approaching sirens again, then back to hers. "Please, they are probably going to pass us if they haven't stopped already", she said as she placed her open palms softly on his cheeks. "They would have started slowing down by now if they were coming here." She pulled his face gently toward hers, until the very tips of their noses touched. "Please".

With this, the killer loosened his grip on her arms and shut his eyes for several seconds. He was still breathing hard, but through his nose as his lips were pressed together. She realized at that moment, he was more afraid than he was angry. The sirens continued to get louder, until it seemed they were right in front of the house. Then they continued pass.

The killer let out a huge sigh of relief and loosened his grip on Sonia's arms to a gentle embrace. He opened his eyes, looking directly into Sonia's again. Still holding his face close, she said, "See, I told ya", with an open smile. The relief she was feeling in that instance was sincere, but for herself.

The killer released Sonia from his grasp and rushed over to the nearby window to see where the cops were finally stopping. From his position, he could see them pulling into her driveway and heading up toward the house. Sonia dropped her hands to her side, her right hand landing on the large can of condensed milk she had dropped in a panic only moments ago. "Okay", he said as he continued to peer frantically through the small window, "once we see them go inside we're going to bolt through the back door and head to the boathouse. It'll take us half the time to drive a boat across the lake than it will take them to drive their cars all the way back around!"

Sonia realized he had not only taken the bait, hook, line, and sinker, but he was totally fixated on the cops. This was her chance.

She clutched the heavy can with both hands and elevated it all the way over her head. She swung her legs forward as hard as she could, lifting herself off the counter and toward the distracted killer, then brought the can down on the crown of his head with all of her might. The man grunted and bowed over the small breakfast table that was between him and the window. Realizing the man was still conscious, Sonia let out an angry shriek as she brought the can down on the back of his head. Then she struck him again, and again. She struck him with all her might until the man was laying on the floor, moaning in pain as he cradled his own head.

Without another wasted breath, Sonia turned and ran as fast as her short legs would take her down the hall toward the living room. She saw the gun lying on the coffee table just as they had left it. In her haste, she tossed the dented can to the side and reached for the gun, grasping it with both hands. She looked toward the hallway expecting to see the man pursuing her, but saw only the faded light from the kitchen against the walls. She then grabbed the top of the gun with her left hand and pulled it back, just as her brother had taught her to do. To her surprise, no bullet flew from the chamber.

This means her brother nor had the killer racked the gun. Had she tried to shoot the gun before racking it, there would have been no gunshot.

As she released the slide, she saw one round go forward into the chamber. Then grasped it with both hands and pointed it toward the hallway prepared to shoot. The hallway was once again empty. Aiming with one hand down the hallway, she used the other to pat down her jacket that was still laid across the armchair for her keys. Sonia was aware that if the keys were not in the jacket pocket still, she would have to shoot the killer in order to get them back.

"Oh, thank God", she shouted as her hand land firmly on the keys through the fabric. She didn't want to risk them falling from her pocket as she ran back toward her house, so she reached in to take them by hand. Just as she pulled them from the jacket, she look up to see the killer standing in the kitchen from the other end of the hallway, glaring at her with the same rage he had just before she convinced him to trust her." Sonia raised the gun back to him. He jumped to the side just as she fired two shots in anger. Perhaps she winged him, but she wasn't going to stick around to find out.

Sonia ran for the door just across from her. She looked over her shoulder for the large man just as she exited. Slamming the door behind her, she ran down the steps toward the bright flashing lights that were the police sirens. She could see several police officers standing between their cars and her house, looking in her direction. They seemed confused, yet alert.

She wasn't sure whether they could see her or not. Sonia was half way through the yard when she heard the front door open, slamming loudly against the wall. She twisted her body as she ran and raised the gun in the direction of the door, firing another two shots in the direction of the killer.

Sonia ran as fast as she could toward the police. "Heeeeyyyyyyy", she yelled to them. "Heeeeellllllllp!!!!" She could hear the police were yelling something back, but she could not make out what they were saying. In fact, she couldn't see where they were, only the cars which were being masked by the spinning bright lights of their sirens.

Sonia could see her body being wrapped in the light of the sirens, she knew the cops could see her. She took one last look over her shoulder to see if she was being pursued. She didn't see the killer anywhere, just the house and yellow light shining through the kitchen window. Sonia was just meters from the police cars now. She was saved! She looked toward the garage and could see the car she had left her daughter in illuminated by the blue light of the police sirens. Her baby would be saved! She saw the silhouette of a police officer's head poking above the open door of the squad car closest to her. As she raised her arms forward and continued to yell toward the man, she could hear the police officer was yelling something as well. Sonia could barely hear him above her own vice.

"Gun, gun, gun", the officer yelled. Just then, Sonia saw several bright yellow flashes erupt from in front of her accompanied by a series of loud popping noises. It felt as though she had been hit by a truck. She felt herself lift from the ground slightly and fly black, her wind completely knocked out. She was looking up at the night sky, clear and littered with brilliant silvery stars. Sonia began choking on her own blood. In her excitement that she experienced from surviving her long, terrifying ordeal, Sonia completely forgot that she was still holding a loaded gun in her hand as she ran toward them frantically yelling. Perhaps they were surprised and confused by the barrage of gunshots coming from the darkness behind them. Perhaps they could only see the muzzle flashes as Sonia shot at her attacker, but could not see the direction the gun was pointing. Perhaps they thought the shots were being fired in their direction. No matter the case, Sonia realized she was dying. She thought of her daughter, her poor Sophia clinging to life in the back of her car. Just meters away from the men that showed up to save her, but cut her mother down. Sonia began drifting into thought, memories of her daughter flooded her mind. Her body was now virtually numb, but Sonia could feel a single warm tear roll from her eye and down toward her ear.

Suddenly, there was a person standing above Sonia pointing a gun down toward her face, looking down, with a stern but confused expression. With one foot he kicked the gun from her hand and shouted over his shoulder, "Suspect down, gun cleared!"

"What's that in her other hand?" a female voice called out from behind the cop standing above her.

"Keys", he shouted in response.

Sonia realized that even though she would not be the one to rescue her daughter, the police still could. She just needed to reveal Sophia's location to them.

"M-mm-y baby", Sonia gurgled through her own thick blood. "My-baby."

The cop's eyes became wide and glassy as he began to make out her wet words. "Shhhit", he whispered, without removing his eyes from hers. "Shit, I think this is Sonia. I think she's the victim! Oh fuck!"

More shouts arose from the officers, but Sonia could not make out their words. They weren't making any sense to her. She realized she was slipping away. Her mind was altered by the feeling of something cold in her limp hand, her keys. It took every bit of strength and focus Sonia had remaining to press her thumb to the panic button. Startled by the unexpected commotion of the car alarm and wilding blinking lights, the police spun in the direction of the car.

"Check that out! The victim hit the panic button, check the car!" the officer above her shouted as he holstered his weapon and dropped to a knee beside her. As he placed his hands on bleeding wounds and began speaking to her, but she couldn't focus on his words. Sonia rolled her head toward the car just in time to see an officer break the rear driver side window, then reach in. "It's the girl, she's alive", he screamed to the others. "She's breathing, she's alive!"

Sonia felt another tear roll down her face as she mustered a faint smile, relieved for her daughter and thankful to God for preserving her life. Just then, Sonia's vision started blurring in and out. Her eyes felt extremely heavy, and her body cold. She laid there on the ground, in the very spot she had stopped just a short while earlier to enjoy the magnificent view. The same spot where she had first laid eyes on the neighboring house closest to her own. The house. With her final bit of energy Sonia rolled her head back toward the house where she spent what seemed like a lifetime of torment. She stared at it in in the distance, a single light lit window presenting yellow light. The same window she noticed as she first laid eyes on it. She looked at the light as her vision faded, and just as quickly as she noticed it, it then suddenly it went out.

STORY TWO

THE HOUSE ON TOP OF THE HILL

It was not always a monster, and it was not always feared. At first, it was merely a creature that lived in the woods, and it belonged to a little girl. She was quite sure that nobody had ever seen it but her. At the library, she tried to find pictures of it in exotic animal books, but she never did.

She first found it in the woods, near a gaping hole in the ground. The little girl was frightened of the hole. The air around it was like ice, and she couldn't see the bottom. She rescued the creature, which was small and seemed as though it must have strayed far from home. It couldn't find food for itself, so she tempted it with bugs and worms she dug out of the ground herself.

But soon, the creature grew larger, and insects were not enough. She bought it mice at the pet store, until it grew larger still, until it was bigger than the biggest dog she had ever seen. It was a great, hulking thing that walked on four legs, but had two long, swirling tentacles with which it grabbed its prey. The little girl didn't know what it ate, alone in the woods. She could no longer find food big enough for it to eat, but it didn't matter. It had learned to take care of itself.

The head of the neighbor's dog was found in its backyard. They never found its body. Then a three-year-old boy went missing, and two weeks later, hunters found his head, torn from his body, out in the woods.

The little went out to the woods and called for the creature, frightened. Would it still know her? Would she be its next victim? But it knew her, and came to her. If it weren't for the little girl, it would have died long ago.

She led it to the top of the hill where she had originally found it. A chill emanated from the hole in the ground, although the day was warm. She had a raw steak she'd stolen from her parent's refrigerator. She threw it into the hole, and the creature, hungry, trusting, dove in after it.

The little girl waited for a while, but the creature didn't come back out. She imagined it hurtling downward through the icy air to whatever lay below. Saddened, she walked away, back down the hill toward the town of Montson. She did not know if she would ever see it again.

Ten Years Later

The house was built on top of a hill. To the west, the new landowners could see the sun setting over forested land and the lake in the distance. To the south, they could see the town of Montson stretched out below, sleepy and quiet. Montson was almost an ideal town, with good schools and very little crime. There was an old legend that it was haunted, because every few years a townsperson seemed to go missing, sometimes with the gruesome remains of its head left behind.

But Mr. and Mrs. Kelling, the new landowners at the top of the hill, weren't worried about the ghost story. Ghost stories were for children, Mr. Kelling said with a loud laugh. A disappearance every few years is nothing to worry about. The Kellings also weren't worried that the land on the top of the hill was so inexpensive. According to the realtor, this was only because of a deep cavity in the ground, right in the center of the property. "Nothing to worry about," she said quickly, when asked. But the hole did make Mrs. Kelling a bit nervous. The air was cold near it, and when she stood on the very edge of it, gripping Mr. Kelling's arm for security, she couldn't even see down to bottom. She wondered if something might be lurking inside.

"Merely an inconvenience," her husband assured her. "We'll make a lowball offer and build here the first day we own the place."

And they did. And for a while, the Kellings were quite happy in the house on top of the hill. They were popular with the townspeople, and were known for throwing elaborate parties in their home. Until one day, two years after they'd moved in. Mr. Kelling had gone down to the basement to measure for a new pool table. It was quite a regular day.

Mrs. Kelling was upstairs, taking a roast out of the oven, singing quietly to herself when she heard it. A long, loud, rip, like a piece of fabric being torn in two. She dropped the roast on the floor, shattering the pan and splattering her dress with gravy.

"D-Don?" she called. "Did you hear that? That ripping sound?" But there was no answer.

"Don? I-I dropped the roast." Still no answer. She opened the basement door, surprised to find that the air was ice cold. The hair on her arms stood on end. "Don?"

When she got to the bottom of the stairs, she let out a bloodcurdling scream. The concrete floor had peeled away from itself to reveal an enormous hole in the ground, the bottom of which she could not see. And at the edge of the hole, splattered with blood, was the head of her husband, Don Kelling, severed from its body as though someone, or something, had ripped it off.

By the end of the year, Mrs. Kelling was gone, and two weeks after that, the house was bulldozed to the ground. "Whatever this is," she told herself "need never happen again."

There was no sign left behind of what had happened to the Kellings. But the Montson children brave enough to ride their bikes up to the property on the hill reported that in the depths of the broken-down foundation, they could still see the hole in the ground, as deep as it had ever been before the Kellings filled it in.

Fifty Years Later

Julie and Robert, a young couple in their late twenties, had lived in their dream house for nearly a year. The house had a big, spacious kitchen, a large, beautiful yard, and four bedrooms that Julie was eager to fill with children, little boys and girls that resembled the old photos of she and Robert that she hung in the hallway upstairs.

The young couple was pleased with their purchase. The house had a lovely view of the town of Montson, although Julie's friends in Montson told her that it used to be better, before the town had sprawled out so much. She was surprised to find that while people were happy to talk about the town itself, nobody could tell her much about the property on top of the hill, now known as 4545 Peters Street. Strangely, though the rest of the town had grown up, the area surrounding their own home at the top of the hill was quite empty.

Only old Mrs. Smith would talk to Julie about the property, though she was often perplexing, as though she knew more than she was willing to let on. "The house itself is only, what, twenty years old?" Mrs. Smith countered. "Montson's been around a lot longer than that, and so has that hill." But suddenly she leaned forward, so close that Julie could feel her breath. "Tell me, though. Have you noticed anything strange about the basement? Any holes? Cracks in the foundation?"

"No, not at all," Julie said, surprised.

But that wasn't completely true, she realized later when she was downstairs looking for boxes. There was something strange about the basement, even if it was just the extra chill in the air down there, and sometimes, a draft. But that was normal for basements, wasn't it? But what bothered Julie the most was that Mrs. Smith was right about the basement floor. There were a few places where the concrete was patched, almost as if there had been a large hole in the floor at one time.

She wondered if there was a problem with the house. Mrs. Smith had almost hinted that something was off about the house, or at least about the basement. And once she'd spoken to the old woman, Julie felt as though she noticed every creak, every moan. Sometimes she felt as if something from the outside was trying to get in, something that caused the draft in the basement and made the hair on her arms stand on end. When it creaked and settled, the house seemed older than its twenty years.

Robert, on the other hand, began spending more and more time in the basement as Julie began to avoid it.

"It'd make a great man cave, babe," he grinned, dragging Julie down to show her his vision. "I'll put theater seating over here, a big screen TV over there..." Julie shivered and followed his gaze, aware that she was standing on the patched part of the concrete. She wondered suddenly if there was anything besides concrete underneath her feet. But she didn't say anything to Robert. "Nothing's under there but dirt and worms," he'd say. "You've been watching too many horror films."

"I don't know about the man cave, honey," she said instead. "Renovations could get expensive, and what if we find out that it's not up to code or something and this turns into some kind of money pit?"

The house let out a long, low CREEAAK as she spoke, and she shuddered in response. Was it her imagination, or had the floor vibrated under her feet? "See, it's like the house is about to fall down around us!"

Robert laughed. "Nah, it's just agreeing with me," he said. "It says, get the biggest TV you can, Robert," he teased. Julie laughed, but still, she stepped off the patched concrete, just in case.

In the end, Julie gave into Robert. "It's your dream house, too," she told him.

"That's right, darling," he said, wrapping her in his arms. "We're going to live here for the rest of our lives."

The construction men came the next day, dragging in their gear and tracking muddy boots through the living room to get to the basement stairs. "Sorry, Jules," Robert said apologetically. "We'll get the carpet cleaners in here next." All day, two men named Joe and Drew demolished and hammered and God knows what else. Julie decided to bake a cake to keep her mind off the basement. She was just about to take it out of the oven when she heard a sound like nothing she'd ever heard before.

It sounded like a long, low, ripping sound, like when her grandmother used to tear fabric along the grain, starting soft but growing to a roar within seconds. "Shit! Get back!" one of the workmen shouted.

"Robert?!" she called, covering her ears with her hands.

He ran into the kitchen. "Are you okay? Did you hear that?"

"Yes! It came from the basement!"

"Everyone all right?" Robert called down the stairs. When he opened the door, Julie was struck by the icy chill in the air. The basement had always been drafty, but it had never felt quite like this.

"Yes sir, for now, anyway. You're going to want to see this. I've never seen anything like it. You might want to bring a sweater, too."

Downstairs, the two workmen were standing and peering down into what had become an enormous hole in the floor, even larger than the area that had originally been patched. It was a wide, gaping hole that led straight down into the earth. Julie gasped and clutched Robert's arm.

"I've never seen anything like it," Drew said again. "You hear that ripping sound?" Joe asked. Julie and Robert nodded. "We heard it too, so loud I thought the house was going to rip right apart. But turns out it was just the hole in the floor."

"Just a hole in the floor?!" Julie said hysterically. "How did it get there?"

"I don't know, ma'am. I don't think it could have been anything we did." Joe turned his back to the hole and gestured to the pile of debris on the floor. "All we've done so far is demolish that interior wall. And, well, see for yourself. The hole's so deep I can't see the bottom. That's been there a long time."

Julie looked back at the hole. He was right. She couldn't see the bottom. Except she could hear something. A grunting, clawing sound. Something was coming toward them from inside the hole.

"There's something in there," Julie breathed fearfully. "Something's trying to get out. "Look out!" she shrieked.

A creature was creeping out of the hole. No, not a creature- a tentacle. Like something you'd expect to see arising from the depths of the ocean, except in this case, it was arising from the depths of the earth, of their very basement. Of their dream house. Joe and Drew jumped back, but Robert, growing paunchy and slow in his married life, wasn't fast enough. The tentacle twisted around his ankles, and pulled him closer and closer to the hole.

"Help!" he shrieked, his face red and panicked. Drew and Joe reached out and grabbed his arm, but already, the tentacle was pulling him toward the edge of the hole, but the tentacle, stronger, threatened to pull them all under. The pungent stink of urine reached Julie's nostrils; Robert had pissed himself.

"Honey!" she cried out. "Hold on!"

"I...I can't hold on any longer!" Drew gasped. But before the words left his lips, the tentacle had yanked Robert into the hole. He was gone.

"Robert!" Julie shrieked. "Do something! What can we do?"

The construction crew stared into the hole, aghast. "We've got to get out of here," Joe said. "It could come back."

"Or we could go down-" She knew the words were foolish, but that thing had gotten Robert.

"Are you mad?" Drew said, shaking his head. "No. We're getting out of here. Ma'am, I don't know what that thing was, but it could be back."

"It got Robert," Julie argued feebly, but before she could finish, they heard a sickening crunching sound, and something was thrown up out of the hole. Julie turned away and vomited onto the floor when she saw what it was: her husband's severed head, bloody and splattered, his body nowhere to be seen.

Upstairs, Julie sat at the table with her head in her hands while Drew made coffee. It's your dream house, too. We're going to live here for the rest of our lives. They had said those words just yesterday, and today Robert was gone.

"It's the curse," Drew muttered to Joe. "We should have known better than to come here. There's a reason why nobody ever wants to do work up here."

"W-what do you mean, curse?" Julie asked, picking up her head.

"Nothing," Joe said firmly. "It's just the old folks in Montson yanking your chain."

Drew shook his head. "You know I'm right. You saw that thing."

"I'm calling the police," Julie said abruptly, getting to her feet. The men exchanged looks but didn't stop her. Trembling, she dialed 9-1-1. "Hello, yes, we've had a...an accident. It's my husband, he, well, there was a construction accident-"

"Construction accident my ass," Joe muttered.

"And now he's dead." Julie paused. "4545 Martin Street, yes, that's right. Yes, the basement. How did you know?"

They waited in silence. Julie tried not to think about Robert's severed head, laying on the cold basement floor. We're going to live here for the rest of our lives. When Officer Frank finally arrived, he joined them in the kitchen, but he wouldn't go downstairs. "No thank you, ma'am."

"No thank you? You're the police?" she said, incredulous. "My husband died down there! Don't you want to investigate, or set up yellow tape, or…"

"This wasn't a murder," he said firmly. "Let me guess what happened here. Your husband was down in the basement, and the floor opened up."

"Well, he went down afterwards, but yes, that's right. The whole floor opened right up. How did you know?"

"Ma'am, here's all you need to know about it. Your husband was never in the basement today."

"But-"

Officer Frank held up a hand. "After I leave, you'll go downstairs and push his head back down into the hole, and say he never came home from work today. We'll put in a missing person's report at the station, and eventually he'll fade away, just like every person who ever disappeared in Montson. Lord knows there's been enough of them over the years."

"And the hole?"

"It don't matter," Officer Frank said. "Patch it, bulldoze it, whatever. It'll open up again. The only question is whether you'll be fool enough to be here to see it."

Before they left, Joe and Drew went downstairs to get their tools. "We'll take care of the, uh, other thing, too," Joe told her. Robert's head, she thought. She imagined it falling down into the hole. Was it a bottomless pit? Would his head fall forever? Or would it reach some other world, some cold, chilly place where that tentacle thing lived? If she jumped into the hole, could she land there, too?

"You should sell this place, ma'am," Drew told her when she walked them out to their truck. "Get far away from here and start over somewhere new."

When they were gone, she sat alone in the living room. This was supposed to be their dream house, hers and Robert's. We're going to live here for the rest of our lives. Here in the living room, on her beautiful white sofa, it was still perfect. Robert could be working in the garage, he could be on his way home work. It's your dream house, too. Could she live here forever, alone? Maybe the thing would never come back.

If Robert were alive, he would be dismissive. "You believe that drivel, Jules? A curse? I'm not selling the place because of a little construction accident that the police don't want to investigate. We'll patch over the hole, it's obviously just a little problem with the foundation."

But Robert was dead.

The next morning, she called around town to find someone to patch the hole. None of the Montson construction companies would take the job, however. A few of them heard the address and hung up the phone. "Maybe Mrs. Smith can recommend someone," Julie wondered, remembering that the old woman had asked about the basement floor.

Julie called Mrs. Smith. ""I'm wondering..." she hesitated. "I'm wondering if you knew the family who lived here before us."

"Todd and Agnes Mitchell," Mrs. Smith said immediately. "Yes, of course. Terribly sad what happened to them."

"What happened?"

"Well, nobody knows for sure, do they?" Mrs. Smith said vaguely. "Some accident or other, though. Agnes went missing. Todd stayed for a while, but he left eventually. They all do."

"What do you mean, they all do?"

Mrs. Smith paused. "Did something happen at the house?"

"Yes," she admitted. "Something did happen. Can you come over?"

"I'll be right over," Mrs. Smith said. "And, if you need a construction crew, Dale's Construction will do the job. Twenty miles down the highway. They won't ask any questions, either. They never do."

By the time Mrs. Smith pulled into the driveway at 4545 Peters St., Julie had already booked Dale's Construction for the next day.

"Who did it take?" Mrs. Smith asked before Julie had even invited her inside. "Your husband?"

"Yes, Robert," Julie said, her eyes filling with tears for the first time. "The police-"

"Oh, pshaw," Mrs. Smith waved her hand impatiently. "They weren't helpful, were they? They know very little, even less than I do. They know that every few years a hole rips through the foundation of this property, and someone from Montson goes missing, usually someone from this very house. If you're lucky, you'll find bits and pieces of them, enough to know they're really gone." She raised an eyebrow at Julie.

"His head," she whispered.

Mrs. Smith nodded. "The police don't know any more than that. In the old days, when the disappearances first happened, they investigated but never found a thing. By the time they learned about the hole, there was nothing they could do. Now they just cover it up. No matter what they do, no matter who's living here or isn't, someone is killed every few years when it comes up to feed."

"How do you know all this?" Julie asked.

Mrs. Smith didn't speak for a long time. "I knew when I first met you that if you lived, I'd tell you the truth," she said finally. "I'm getting old, you see. There's no point in keeping the secret anymore. It's been over sixty years since I last saw the creature that took your husband."

"You've seen it? And it didn't...it didn't kill you?"

"I'm the one who found it first, when I was just a child. I don't know what's at the other end of that hole, but I know that it came out of it. I could have killed the creature when I found it, but instead, I helped it live. It was so small then, so dependent on me. I didn't tell a soul. By the time I knew what it had become, I told myself it was too late, but the truth was, that I didn't want them to kill it. Men would come with guns and with God knows what else, and they'd kill it or take it away. I didn't want it to die. I didn't want anyone to die."

She paused for so long that Julie thought she had fallen asleep.

"When the Kellings bought the property back in 1950, I breathed a sigh of relief. Several people had gone missing by then, and I thought that if the Kellings filled the hole and built a house, then the thing won't be able to get out. That tunnel to wherever it's from would be sealed off, and we'd be free. But then Mr. Kelling disappeared, and Mrs. Kelling left town, and I knew that it would never end. I've lived in Montson all my life, and all my life I've known that someone would be next. This time it was your husband, and if you don't leave, it'll be you, too."

But Julie didn't leave. Whether or not this was a surprise to anyone in Montson, she didn't know. Nobody asked any questions. Nobody in Montson ever did. It was as though Robert had never existed. We're going to live here for the rest of our lives.

A year passed, then two, then three. Julie went home to her dream house at the end of every day. She never went down into the basement.

One day, when she got home from her job at the bank, Mrs. Smith was sitting on the doorstep, waiting. "It's time," she said. "Three years have passed. It'll be back again."

"Maybe it won't come this time," Julie said, unlocking the door. She sounded like Robert, a skeptic. "Maybe it's dead, or gone, or last time was enough."

"I've been telling myself that for sixty-three years, but it always comes back. But I know what to do now."

"You can't do that," Julie said a half hour later. "It's suicide."

"Either you leave, and it comes and takes someone else, or eventually it takes you, too. I'm an old woman. I don't have much time left. Let me be the one, and then you can leave for good. And who knows….maybe it will remember me. Maybe that will be enough, and we can put this to rest."

"How do we know when it will come?"

Mrs. Smith reached into her bag and pulled out an old, battered leather journal. "I've recorded every instance I could learn of where a person disappeared in Montson. Every third October, it comes, and often, when the family is in the basement. It's drawn to the activity when it's ready to feed." She opened to the first page. "The Kellings, with their pool table, for example."

"Robert's construction crew," Julie nodded.

"Yes. And six years ago, Agnes Mitchell was exercising on her new treadmill, down in the basement."

"It's suicide," Julie said again.

"Maybe. But I want to see it once more before I die."

One week later, Mrs. Smith and Julie sat together in the living room. Julie flipped through the journal, reading the names.

Margaret Winters, age 32.

Gerald Montgomery, age 65.

Monica Anderson, age 7.

She swallowed hard. It was always the third week of October. Mrs. Smith had almost always been able to confirm that some member of the family had been in the basement when the hole opened up. In a few cases, the house had been unoccupied, and the creature had ventured out of the house and down the hill, into the town of Montson, where it found even more unsuspecting prey.

Julie shuddered, thinking of the creature creeping through the town, sliding its tentacles around the corner to grab an unsuspecting victim before returning back to its lair.

"Did the victims lose their...I mean, were they decapitated right there, when they were kidnapped in town?" Julie asked. It was gruesome, the thought of a head left without a body in the middle of a blood-splattered sidewalk. She imagined Robert's head, lying in the lawn, herself going out in the morning and finding it there.

"I don't think so," Mrs. Smith said delicately. "I never heard of a head being found outside of the home. Always in the basement. I think it took its victims alive, dragged them up the hill and back to the house. I don't know that anyone ever saw it either, but of course, this is Montson. Who would say something if they had?"

Julie shivered. Somehow the victim being carted off alive was worse than the instant decapitation she had pictured. Even Robert had only suffered a few terrifying moments before he died. Julie pushed away the thought of her husband's head rolling at her feet, and looked instead at the old woman in front of her.

"I don't think you should do it, Mrs. Smith. I think...I think you should leave. Maybe we should both leave, we could go away together." Even as she said it, she knew she wouldn't do it. She felt as tied to her dream house as Mrs. Smith did to the monster itself.

The old woman looked down at the journal and didn't respond. "I'm feeling a little peckish, Julie," she said at last. "Could you perhaps scrape together a little lunch for us?"

Julie nodded. Perhaps after lunch, she could talk the old woman out of this madness, this suicide mission. She went into the kitchen and pulled out the bread and lunch meat and began assembling some sandwiches. She poured two glasses of orange juice, and went into the living room. Nobody was there.

"Mrs. Smith?" she called. "Hello?"

Mrs. Smith was nowhere to be seen. But, Julie realized with a sinking feeling in her stomach, the basement door was open. "Oh no," she breathed.

And then, she heard it. The same sound she had heard three years ago. The same sound Mrs. Kelling and Gerald Montgomery and little Monica Anderson, and so many others had heard during the years. It started quietly, like the sound of someone ripping fabric, and grew louder and louder until Julie dropped the glasses of orange juice and covered her ears. She ran through the broken glass to the open basement door.

Mrs. Smith was standing on the bottom step, looking down into the basement, where the hole had opened up once again. "No!" Julie screamed. "Come back upstairs!"

"It's too late, Julie!" The old woman's voice rippled with a perverse excitement. "It'll be here any moment! Stay back!"

As their eyes adjusted to the darkness, they saw the first tentacle emerge from the hole in the floor. Julie wanted to run, but she was frozen in place, watching the thing that killed her husband return for what could easily have been Julie herself. A second tentacle emerged from the hole when the first one didn't find an easy target. Standing on the stairs, Mrs. Smith was too far back, Julie realized. The old woman didn't know what happened when her creature emerged from the hole. She had never seen it kill.

The monster pulled itself up by its tentacles. Julie could see very little of it in the darkness, only its glowing green eyes and its tentacles, now reaching for Mrs. Smith on the stairs.

"Oh...oh my," Mrs. Smith murmured. "My darling, how big you have grown."

The monster paused, its green eyes fixed upon the old woman who had once given it life. "I've come back for you," she whispered. "Do you know me, my pet?"

Julie held her breath, waiting. The creature withdrew its tentacles for barely a moment before it lashed out again and grabbed the old woman, dragging her back toward the hole.

"No!" Julie screamed. The monster turned back toward her, noticing her for the first time. For a split second, its eyes met hers, green and narrow like a cat's in the darkness. Her heart pounded. She imagined it dropping Mrs. Smith and climbing the stairs. Did it prefer younger meat to older? Or were two victims better than one?

But it did not. It plunged into the hole, dragging its elderly prey with it. Julie was left alone, standing on the steps in the icy air.

Later, Julie turned on the light and ventured down into the basement, carefully avoiding the edge of the hole. She could see her breath in the cold air. She grabbed a broom handle and tried not to retch as she pushed Mrs. Smith's ancient head into the hole. She listened for it to hit the bottom, but didn't hear a sound.

She closed the door and went back upstairs, where she picked up Mrs. Smith's journal and slid it carefully, reverently under her mattress. Eventually, she would add a new entry under Robert's name.

She didn't call the police, and she didn't call Dale's Construction, either. In a few days, people would notice the absence of Mrs. Smith around town, but nobody would ask questions. Nobody in Montson ever did.

In three years, there would be another disappearance in the house at the top of the hill.

Nobody would ask questions. Nobody in Montson ever did.

STORY THREE

BURIED IN A CLOSET

PROLOGUE

Sarah placed her palms on her mouth and held her breath. Her body had frozen, unable to comprehend what next to do as she hid in the closet. She knew she had a ten percent chance of ever living to see the next morning but she hoped she would. There was so much that she wanted to tell the police about who the murderer was.

Who he was and what he became when no one was watching.

She could see everything that was happening in the bedroom through the tiny holes on the closet doors. Two minutes ago, the entire room had been filled with dreadful screams as he killed everyone – every single adult and every child. Apart from her, there were three other people in the house and he had murdered everyone at cold blood.

He had murdered her entire family and now, he was looking for her.

She didn't know how he did it or where he drew his strength from. The only thing she could comprehend from the blood that dripped from throats as he swiftly moved about in the shadows of the room was that he didn't have a conscience anymore. She had had to watch everything without muttering a word. At a time, her brother's head had left his body and had come flying towards the closet. She had been compelled to scream at the top of her voice but the need to survive had clipped her lips shut instead.

She needed to find a way to escape.

The room and the entire house had been silent for over five minutes now – ten minutes to be precise. She didn't have her phone with her nor was she wearing her wristwatch but the passage of time really mattered to her as she found somewhere to hide. She had begun to count the figures in her head as soon as the screams stopped and the sound of his footsteps on the blood-filled rugs reduced.

She was safe. She was safe. She was safe… as long as she stayed in the closet and made no sound.

Checking through the holes again, Sarah glanced round the room, checking for any signs of movement. The room was as still as the air and the blood on the floor and the walls wasn't going to dry up soon. She could see the lifeless body of everyone on the floor, counting only two. The first victim's body was lying downstairs, at the sitting room.

She had seen everything as it happened and she was still alive!

Suddenly, her vision of the room was blurred as someone swiftly moved in front of the closet. Her palm flew to her mouth again and it took all the strength in her body to stop the scream from leaving her throat.

He could see her. He knew where she was. She could feel his cold murderous stare on the closet and finally on her. It was as if his eyes could see through the doors deep into her own eyes. She felt the hunger in his eyes; the hunger to draw her out and end her life too. Afraid beyond control, Sarah closed her eyes and became as still as the fabrics in the closet.

He is going to reap me into two, spill my blood all over and drag my intestines all around the floors of the house!

Sarah didn't know where the image in her head came from but she had seen him doing worse when the killings started. He could have worse plans for her once he found out that she had hidden somewhere just to escape him.

"It is okay Sarah. You can come out now… There isn't any point hiding in there all night."

Her eyes fluttered open as the familiar voice reeked throughout the small walls of the closet. He wasn't in there with her but she could feel the raw power of his rage and the compelling influence of his voice.

Don't step out Sarah. Don't!

The choice wasn't hers anymore. She felt the need to step out and run for her life. She felt as if she was safer out of the closet than in it. Her body was restless. Her teeth began to grit together, almost digging into the soft flesh of her lips. She was prepared for whatever was waiting for her in the room. Her legs would carry her as far away as it could. He would catch up with her but she was going to make him sweat first.

Heaving a long sigh, Sarah opened the door and slowly stepped out, intending to reach towards the door immediately he came after her.

Nothing happened. The room was dimly lit and absolutely still. He was gone!

Having no intention to debate if he was really gone or not, Sarah ignored the sickness in her stomach as she glanced around at the blood and dead bodies and began to flee. Her heart began to beat faster as soon as she left the hall and began to take the stairs to the large sitting room downstairs. There was blood everywhere and it made her dizzy and nauseous. She wanted to puke but the need to survive took care of that for her.

She finally crossed the sitting room and made it to the front door. She was right; a feet away from the door was her mother's dead body. Her eyes were widely opened, filled with shock and confusion. He had been gentle with her; he had only slit her throat and had left her entire body intact. The rest hadn't been so lucky.

"Saraaaaaah!" The house suddenly echoed, shaking her thoughts.

Sarah forgot about her dead mother immediately and reached for the handle of the door, hoping to escape into the cold night. She had high hope now that she might actually get to see the next light in the sky.

The lock didn't budge.

She turned just in time to see the shadows around the sitting room shifting from one end to another. Footsteps began to echo down the stairs as he came for her. This was fun to him; he wanted her to run first and when she was exactly where he wanted her to be, he would end her life.

He was getting closer.

Finally, when the air around her whizzed with his movement and his stench filled her nostrils, Sarah plastered her back on the door and opened her mouth to scream. No sound left her lips though as her throat swiftly began to gasp on her own blood. Her body froze first before it fell towards the floor like a heavy lump. She was choking on her own blood afterwards and she didn't know what to do.

In that brief moment before she lost control of her body, her hand reached forward and grabbed his ankle. He didn't move. He simply stood there and glanced down at her as if he admired her resilience. His blood-filled eyes began to move closer as he crouched to stare at her. She felt his fingers on her hair afterwards as if he was soothing her to sleep. Eventually, Sarah gasped her last breath and closed her eyes.

Everywhere became dark afterwards.

Ten Years Later

It was past midnight by the time he got to the murder scene.

An hour ago, he had been woken up by a phone call from his partner, Alexis Willow, and Alexis hadn't said anything much except that there was a murder case on the outskirt of Broad Street and he had to get his ass there pronto. He couldn't argue with her about how late it was though since they had been together on the job for almost five years. Waking up in the middle of the night and driving to some murder scene had always been a part of their job.

He had only jumped to the bathroom and sprinkled water on his face before hopping into his car and driving thirty minutes to the address that Alexis had given him.

Detective Malfoy Bordeaux was at the murder scene now and he wished that he was somewhere else instead. The entire family in the house had been insanely murdered and their bodies had been hurdled together in the middle of the house. Two female bodies were completely naked and was filled with their own blood while the third victim was male. His body had been dragged from the door to the middle of the house though, just beside the other two, and his clothes were soaked with blood. He was also missing an arm.

The killer, whoever it was, had slit their throats, their wrist and had placed them on top each other as if doing that would help their poor soul.

Alexis, seeing the expression on his face as soon as he stepped into the four-bedroom bungalow, had shaken her head and had pointed to the passage that led to the nearest bedroom.

"There is more?" he asked her.

Alexis nodded and began to walk towards the bedroom. He imagined that the scene had been so horrific to her too that she couldn't mutter any word. Why the family built their house quite distant from the busy city streets aroused his curiosity though – they could have screamed for help all they wanted and their nearest neighbor would have thought it was the wind playing tricks on him. Before Detective Malfoy stepped into the house, he had seen the tiny dot of another house just like the bungalow a field-distance or so away.

"You should hold your breath." Alexis warned him before slowly opening the door.

At first, Detective Malfoy didn't understand what she meant as he glanced around the poorly-lit room. He stepped further into the room afterwards, noticing for the first time that the red bed sheet wasn't supposed to be red. The entire material had been soaked with blood that it was almost difficult to note that it used to be plain white.

"The females in the sitting room had been killed here and drained of all their blood." Alexis noted, speaking for the first time.

Detective Malfoy nodded, noting the same thing.

"This isn't what you want me to see, is it?" He asked her, having a feeling that Alexis was reluctant to even step beyond the door.

"Check the closet." She whispered behind him.

Detective Malfoy felt compelled to roll his eyes at her but he could always do that after they were through investigating the occurrence in the house. He had left the forensic agents in the sitting room and they would be in the bedroom too any time soon. Alexis must have saved the details of the bedroom as last for them as she had for him too.

"Just open it Malf." Alexis sighed behind him.

Wanting to get it over with too, Detective Malfoy slowly reached for the handle of the closet and pulled the shutters open.

The sight that greeted him almost stopped the beating of his heart.

"Oh my God." He gasped.

The entire city forensic team had been called in for this one. The murder was gruesome and the police department weren't only sick with the sights, they were furious and needed answers before morning.

Sarah moved around the house, blending in with the state department uniform that had been hers for the past few years. What she saw appalled her but it wasn't something that she hadn't seen before. It reminded her of a very long time ago; of a time when she had almost died at the entrance of her parents' house, clutching tight the feet of her murderer.

She was in the first bedroom of the house now where it was obvious that the madness had begun. According to what she had seen so far, the murderer had played the same peekaboo game with the family, killing the first victim at the door, and getting the rest of the family in one single room for a mass slaughter. He had saved the youngest child by allowing her to hide in the closet. This time around, he didn't have the time to let her try to escape. He had mutilated the poor girl's body in the closet, smashing her entire bones with something heavy. Sarah's guess was a heavy iron mallet, which the killer had probably taken with him when he left the house and disappeared into the night.

The poor child in the closet hadn't played the game well the same way Sarah had ten years ago.

Sarah sighed, figuring that she had seen enough. The entire room smelled of death and blood and no one – not even if the forensic scientist was the best in the world – was going to figure out who the killer was. He was that good. He had destroyed her home once and she was only alive for this long because he wanted it that way. She wouldn't be surprised if he was amongst the officers that was busy hurrying around the house, pretending to be helping the law enforcement carry out their research.

If he was, then this wasn't over yet; more people were going to die. She had changed her name once and had erased everything about her past, Sarah thought. Once everything went south again, she was going to disappear again. She had bled out and died once at the feet of a mad man; she wasn't about to go through that horror again.

The police were going to meet a dead end with this one the same way they had with her family ten years ago.

He had smashed her head with a very heavy mallet.

Detective Malfoy sat at his desk eight hours later staring at the picture of the slain family and the report from the forensic team. He had only been able to sleep for an hour or two before the forensic team had dropped a report on his desk as soon as there was light in the sky. The report had confirmed everything he had suspected about the body in the closet. She was young, very young, and despite the way that the murderer had disfigured her body with a mallet, the team had been able to determine her age as seventeen or eighteen.

Damn!

He felt like getting his hands on the murderer and hit him hard his nose would bleed forever. He wasn't close to figuring who it was though. The entire murder scene had been completely empty of any foreign finger print. The family members had been identified as Henry Winfred, the father who had been killed at the door and was dragged to join his wife, Mary and their first daughter, Shirley. The youngest daughter was allowed to hide in the closet before she was killed in a more horrible manner.

Hell!

Cursing wasn't going to solve the case for him, Detective Malfoy knew this. It was just so difficult to accept the truth that the killer had been so perfect with the killings that he was impossible to trace. Someone needed to be caught for the heinous act!

"I found something!"

Detective Malfoy almost jumped out from his chair with joy as Alexis rushed into the office, flipping a file at him.

"Ten years ago murder." She grinned, "Almost the same act. The same way of huddling the victims together. I had the team dig up any case that was similar to this one just to get us a few tips on how to catch the murderer!"

"What are you talking about?" Detective Malfoy asked, collecting the file from her and checking through the police report in it.

"The murderer was never found as well?" he asked her, already flipping through the pages.

"Yes." Alexis muttered. "He killed almost everyone in the house."

"Almost?" Detective Malfoy asked.

He already flipped enough to see the pictures of the family that had been murdered too. There was a young boy – younger than the latest victim in the closet – that had been killed beside the closet too. His head had been cut off from his body. Closing the file with a sigh, Detective Malfoy stared at Alexis with a questioning stare.

"The father survived." She muttered.

"He did?"

Why did that surprise him? He thought murderers that mutilated their victims never left survivors.

"Yeah. He did." Alexis muttered again, "And I found him."

"So fast?" Alexis sure took the case personal than he did. "Have you slept at all?"

Her eyelids did seem heavy as she grinned at him and went over to her table. He still found it odd that they shared an office since they became partners though. That had been partly his fault since the department knew him to love working alone. Sharing an office with her was to force him to get used to working with her without a choice.

"I didn't have to look far." Alexis said, already wearing her badge and placing her gun in its hostler, "he was waiting for us quite where we wouldn't expect him to be."

"You mean the survivor ten years ago?"

"Yes. He is the owner of the only house beside the murder scene. He called to report the crime as well."

This jolted Detective Malfoy to his feet again. He remembered that he had noticed the house quite distant from the Winfred family's bungalow and had inquired if the owner had been questioned. The team had only passed him the statement that the owner had made which only stated something about hearing screams and being unable to do anything but call the police.

"You coming?" Alexis asked, already moving towards the door.

Heck, if he wasn't heading to the house right now without her saying anything. Detective Malfoy swore again under his breath and picked up his badge as well.

This was something better than the report that the forensic team had given him. There was nothing in that file except for pictures and the details of an entire family that had been killed in cold blood.

The other house was a field distance from the deceased family's bungalow. Detective Malfoy parked his car just a few feet from the verandah of the house and slowly walked over to the door with Alexis, staying sharp. They hadn't concluded if the owner of the house was the killer yet but there was nothing wrong if they approached the man with extra caution.

Detective Malfoy knocked thrice before the door finally creaked open. A man on a wheelchair appeared at the door, staring at both of them with a curious look.

"Mr. Clark Littleton?" Alexis asked.

The man wheeled himself out to join them and took Alexis hand.

"It has been a long time I answered to that name." he said cheerfully. "It is Lionel Luthor now."

"After the comic book character?" Detective Malfoy asked, taking Lionel's hand too. "I am Detective Malfoy and this is Alexis, my partner."

Lionel laughed and shook his head, "I didn't think of that when I changed the name. What can I do you for, detectives?"

"We have a few questions about your family, Clark....uh, Lionel." Alexis deliberately mentioned his previous name to see his reaction.

Lionel blinked bleakly though, shaking his head as if he didn't understand her.

"I don't have a family." He muttered, "I live here alone. I would have invited you inside for coffee if I didn't."

"You live here alone?" Detective Malfoy asked, interrupting Alexis before she could ask another question, "How do you get things around here done considering...."

He glanced at Lionel's missing legs and let the rest of the question hang in the air.

Again, Lionel didn't flinch. He only smiled and pointed at the Winfred bungalow.

"Apart from sweet Gabrielle, my maid that comes in every weekend, the family over there help me once in a while; that is before they were murdered of course. I called the police that night when I heard screams. It wasn't that audible but I know a scream when I hear one."

"Because you once had a house that was filled with screams while you're entire family was killed?" Alexis asked.

"Alexis..." Detective Malfoy cautioned, preferring to question Lionel about that in a less direct way.

"It is okay Detective." Lionel sighed, turning to face Alexis, "Yes, I lost my family once and none of the men in uniform were able to find the killer. If you are here to ask me if I knew the killer, you are doing nothing that hasn't been done ten years ago. It was horrible waking up and finding your legs dislodged from your body. I changed my name and moved on. If the same thing is happening with another family, I have nothing to do with it and I don't want to be a part of it."

Detective Malfoy tried to detect any real pain, remorse or fear in Lionel's voice but the man only spoke nonchalantly. His eyes moved from dropped to the floor while he began to wheel back towards the door of his home.

"I guess that answers all the unasked questions?" Lionel whispered, pausing at the door.

"You didn't get to see the murderer?" Detective Malfoy asked, wanting to confirm that.

"Yes." Lionel sighed. "The last thing I remembered was sleeping beside my wife and waking up at the door, bleeding from my thighs. I never knew how I got there."

Detective Malfoy glanced at Alexis and noticed that she was as disappointed as he was too. Coming to question Lionel was also a dead end. The man had been a victim of a mad man too, if the two murder cases wasn't entirely different.

"Alright. Thanks for your time, Lionel." Detective Malfoy said, already heading down the verandah with Alexis.

"Detective Malfoy?" Lionel whispered behind them.

He was inside the house now and had wheeled around to stare at them. His gaze stayed long on Alexis first before it focused on Detective Malfoy, staying there.

"If it was the same murderer that came after my family. I suggest that you both don't pursue him. You might be heading towards something that you would never understand. I don't sleep at night, but at least I am still alive."

The door closed before either of them could say anything. That felt like a sincere warning and it was the first time that Lionel spoke with a bit of emotion. Detective Malfoy had detected a hint of concern in his voice and it sure made his heart miss a beat.

Clark Littleton might have changed his name to Lionel Luthor, but his past still haunted him. There was something about his last statement that made it seem like Lionel was afraid that an unknown murderer in his past would be coming for him again.

He needed to dig a little further into Lionel's past, he thought silently to himself.

————

Lionel Luthor.

Clark Littleton shook his head at the name that he had thought could protect him forever. The second bottle of born bourn was right in front of him, compelling him to keep drinking until his life ended as it should have ten years ago.

It was night already and he had gotten the message quite clear yesterday when the Winfreds were killed. The murderer of his family had found him, despite shifting home numerous times over the years. He didn't have to be in the house before he knew how each one of them was killed. There would have been bodies piled up in the middle of the room and then the last body would be inside or near to the closet.

That was how the murderer worked. That was how Clark had thought him to think.

Clark downed another cup of the hot drink and groaned aloud, cursing his life. Everything had been perfect the first few years when he married Clarisse, his wife, but his life had changed when they started having children. He never thought of having children but he didn't hate any of those Clarisse bore for him. Their children were beautiful as kids and he had adored them, watching them as they grew.

It wasn't until the oldest was eight years old that everything changed.

Sighing, Clark filled another cup and began to wheel himself to his bedroom. He knew he wasn't alone in the house anymore but he didn't care. He simply watched as the shadow behind him began to move with him, crossing the hall and following him to the bedroom.

"You always did know how to enter the house without getting the door to make any sound." Clark muttered, wheeling round to stare at his nemesis.

"I learnt everything from you." The voice was exactly as Clark could remember it.

"You didn't have to kill them you know." Clark whispered.

"Of course I didn't." came the response with a very long chuckle, "but I had to make sure you got the message."

"What message?" Clark asked, getting irritated.

"That I only waited this long to do it all over again. To kill everyone that mattered to you the same way you killed everyone that mattered to me. You cared about your new neighbors and killing them was just right."

There was a long silence as Clark stared through the darkness of the room at the only person he ever cared about after his wife. He wondered where everything ever went wrong.

"I didn't kill anyone. You killed everyone and made it up in your head that I did!"

"You are saying it again." The voice was furious now and it was getting closer, "You think I am mad!"

Clark shook his head and wheeled himself forward. He was about to die anyway, he might as well tell his killer everything he wanted to hear.

"You were sick!" Clark shouted, "You were always having multiple personalities and the only way to help you was to meddle with your mind and tell you to choose one personality and kill the rest. I didn't tell you to kill everyone like a lunatic!"

A sharp pain hit the side of Clark's head before he could finish. He had said enough and he just wanted to get this over with. Instead of keeping shut, he raised his voice again.

"You killed everyone! I thought you to lock the other personalities in a closet. I didn't tell you to lock your brother there and cut off his head. You killed them all!"

"Shut up!"

A sharp pain hit his head again, rendering him motionless. As Clark saw a sharp blade coming towards his neck, this time with a very quick motion, he raised his head and laughed heretically, muttering the last words he could think of.

"You are a murderer Sarah. You are still sick!"

Clark Littleton used to be a celebrated psychologist in Oxford. He fell in love with and married one of his patients, Clarisse O'Shea – she used to suffer double personalities and Clark helped her out somehow. They had two children (a boy and a girl) but for years, there wasn't any public record of the girl, Sarah Littleton. Rumors had it that he kept her in a basement as a patient – one that he couldn't crack – for years. It was never revealed what was really wrong with her. When everyone was found dead and Clark barely survived, the daughter wasn't found and it was assumed that she must have died a long time ago but Clark never reported it.

A basement wasn't found in the house as well.

Clark is the primary suspect for her disappearance while the murderer of his entire family still remain at large.

Detective Malfoy was driving at full speed towards Clark Littleton's home. He had immediately gotten a team to find out everything about him after their little encounter in the morning. The team had reported back an hour ago with a background report on him that had shed light on the entire case.

A psychologist? A mysterious daughter who had disappeared? Why the hell didn't anyone just look for Sarah Littleton instead of assuming that she was dead? He suspected that Sarah couldn't have been labelled as a murderer since she was supposed to be sixteen at the time. If he wasn't a detective with lots of experience with murder cases, he would have easily said that all killers were supposed to be adult. Sarah should be twenty-six now and could be anywhere.

She could goddamn be the killer that he was looking for!

He had been dialing Alexis' number immediately he left the office but it had been switched off. Leaving a message that she should meet up at Clark's home anytime soon, Detective Malfoy parked his car beside the house and slowly advanced towards the porch.

Something was wrong. The entire house was dark and the door was slightly opened.

"Dr. Clark Littleton?"

Quickly pulling out his weapon, Detective Malfoy slowly pushed the door wide open and advanced into the house. It was extremely quiet inside and the only source of light in the house was the burning fire at the chimney and the small lamp that lit the small passage to the bedroom.

"Lionel." Detective Malfoy tried again.

Nothing. There weren't any sounds in the house and the door of the first room was slightly opened as well. Something still wasn't right.

Detective Malfoy froze immediately he stepped into the bedroom, almost staggering back. At the middle of the room, on his wheelchair, was Clark Littleton – or what was left of his marred body. Blood oozed from different holes on his body, dripping all over his wheelchair and to the floor. His eyes had been dug out too while his jaw hung loosely to the side.

"What the hell!"

Detective Malfoy wasn't fast enough. The pain hit his chest too fast before he could raise his hands to aim. Someone had been waiting for him in the shadows of the bedroom, bidding their time. The gun dropped from his hands as his body slumped forward, resting on the body of his assailant. The next pain hit his spinal cord before his assailant turned his body around and pushed him to the floor.

"You should have listened to him." His assailant whispered, slowly stepping away from him and reaching for the switch of the table lamp. "You shouldn't have done any extra digging or come back here."

The light came on in the room and Detective Malfoy's eyes widened with shock. His assailant and Clark's murderer was grinning down at him, shaking her head. She was entirely covered in Clark's blood and was holding a very sharp knife in her gloved hand.

"Alexis?" Detective Malfoy managed to whisper, trying to raise himself up.

She had punctured his heart and had dug deep into his backbone. His entire body failed him every time he tried to raise himself up.

"It is Sarah this time around." Alexis muttered, kneeling beside him.

Detective Malfoy was gradually finding it hard to breathe. He glared at Alexis and wondered why he had missed it. She was at the murder scene before any of the team, reporting there immediately Clark put a call through about the screams from the house. Alexis had also dug out files about the murder ten years ago within a few hours. She had found Clark in no time too, for a man that had changed his name and his location quite a number of time.

"I am surprised you missed it too." Alexis was whispering now, reading his mind, "Clark Littleton wouldn't stop staring at me while we questioned him in the morning. The old man wasn't even sure if I looked like his daughter or I was his daughter!"

Her soft laughter managed to echo in the room, sending a mild irritation down his throat.

"Why don't I summarize everything for you before easing your pain?" Alexis whispered, fondling with the knife in her hand.

She pointed to Clark's body and grinned, "One thing about crazy fathers and their offspring. He never locked me in a basement you know? It was always the closet. To him, he was showing me how to cure myself. He wanted me to end a part of me that I never understood. Kill them he often shouted. Bury them in a closet. Kill them and gather the personalities as one."

"So, you decided one day and decided to kill everyone, hurdling them together." Detective Malfoy groaned.

"Oh, I only did what he asked. Mum allowed him to treat me like I never existed but I was gentle with her. I only slit her throat. Jamie, my brother, taunted me all day too, peeping into the closet and shaking his head at me. It was fun finally having to cut that head off."

"I sometimes have jumbled thoughts and realities though." Alexis stood and shook her head as if she was trying to figure something out, "Sometimes, I felt as if I was in the closet at the same time that I killed everyone. I feel as if I was dying in my own pool of blood, murdered by someone I knew too well. It was always me. It was me! Crazy, right?" she was groaning and chuckling at the same time.

Detective Malfoy could only stare at her, wondering how he never suspected anything strange about her. She played the detective so well the whole department was fooled by it.

"Okay, that's enough." Alexis muttered, rushing towards him and sliding the edge of the knife through his throat in a single movement.

"I finally figure it out." He heard her whisper a few seconds later as he began to choke on his own blood.

"I am sick. I am sick. I should have ended this a long time ago."

Detective Malfoy watched as Alexis slowly backed against the nearest wall and sat on the floor, dropping the knife. He saw blood slowly flowing from her wrist as tears slowly began to slide down her cheeks.

She had slit her own wrist.

Detective Malfoy's vision was becoming blurry as his eyelids heavily clasped together. It was only a matter of time before his heart stopped beating too.

The entire city police wasn't ever going to solve this one.

STORY FOUR

THE DEBTS WE PAY

The clock stroke four times near the stairwell as the light from the moon was falling through the window, creating a hardly visible tree outline on the floor, animated by the gently blowing of the wind. Alex and Jason were out cold after a bustling day at work. Their jobs sucked the life's energy out of their marriage with Jason being an archaeologist and she as a writer, both successful in their fields but after four years of marriage instead of being the happy couple that they started out as, it was all about their careers and putting food on the table. They had no children and Alex didn't want to try anymore because of the last two miscarriages that she went through. Those events ripped through their marriage like razor sharp nails, destroying their communications lines with one another; leaving them with a carcass of what used to be.

The sound of footsteps in the stairwell made the floorboards creek and cry out at the strain of some weight on its old wooden surface and Alex to stir in her sleep. In her mind she was awake but her body was still asleep in that moment. There was no one there in the house except for her and Jason. Thoughts of an intruder came to her head but for some strange reason she couldn't move. Alex was really beginning to wonder if she was just having some freaky nightmare and that's the reason why she couldn't wake up.

For a fraction of a minute there was silence. The footsteps had stopped and the house felt as peaceful as it should be at night.

Then, she heard the silent footsteps again. No matter what she did she couldn't get her eyes to open! Thinking about that for a moment, she wondered if this was a blessing, would she want to see the face of whosoever was coming up to their bedroom? Did she want to know what will happen to her or Jason? Her curiosity won the battle over fear and her eyes open quickly but she still couldn't move her body. It was as if there was something holding her in place, paralyzing her with invisible chains that she just couldn't get loose from. Alex tried the next best thing which was to warn Jason, who was blissfully snoring beside her but as she opened her mouth, she found that it was not functioning either.

Shit! The thought rang through her head and bounced like an echo.

In their bedroom, the bed was facing the door and the footsteps sounded like they were coming from that direction. Alex had never been a believer in things that she couldn't see and touch and as for the supernatural, she left that up to Jason. However, what she saw woke her up as if she just downed five cups of coffee all at once. Her eyes grew wide, and her heart started to beat twice as fast as if she just ran a marathon.

The bedroom was dark with only the weak moon light that spilled from the window on the left side, but Alex saw the clear blueprint of some kind of humanlike creature as it came through the bedroom door as if the wood barrier didn't exit and she felt the bed dip as it sat on her side, scanning the room with the silent observation of a stranger.

Its exhaled breaths came out like a fog through its nostrils and then it turned its head for Alex to see it clearly. The top part of its body met the weak moonlight, revealing a white bony skull and a sharp looking horn. Fear was stronger than anything and Alex found her voice and immediately started screaming at the top of her lungs. The ugly creature grinned at her before it stood up and stepped to the shadows near the door.

"What the hell is going on?" A frightened Jason asked.

Alex didn't answer him, she was too terrified, and her eyes never left the figure in the dark that kept grinning at her; enjoying the taste of her fear on his lips and the music of her thundering heart.

There were three things that came Jason's mind in that moment when he tried to ascertain why his wife was screaming her head off.

One. She wasn't looking at him at all but over at the door.

Two. The room was much colder than it should be and it was mid-summer.

And three. He couldn't move.

"I can't move!" He cried out in horror.

Alex didn't stop screaming, she didn't even look at Jason, engrossed in his own shock.

She caught breath for a few seconds and then continued shrieking.

"That's it." The low voice spoke for the first time.

"Scream for me, woman! Fear me!" He added slowly, graciously and in the same way, he emerged from the shadows into the view of the couple.

Without warning the creature came out from the shadow and right before their eyes changed into a human. Jason couldn't believe his eyes, neither could Alex. Whatever air she had left in her screaming reserve dried up when she witness the creatures transformation. She couldn't say anything at that point even if she wanted to. Not with the terror that gripped her tongue. It was Jason that asked the questions that she couldn't.

"Who-Who are you?" he asked in a trembling voice.

"Do you want money? It's downstairs, behind the clock!" he disclosed without hesitation. He, of course wanted this, whatever it was to be over. But he was clearly fear stricken as well.

The creature returned to his observation post, this time looking at the bed-ridden couple with a blank expression on his human face. Then with his long slim fingers, he brushed his now, short dark thick hair, behind his ears and wet his lips. He was wearing a funeral black suit and black shirt underneath to match.

All of them were silent for a few moments before the creature spoke again.

"You humans are so..." he paused for a moment as if thinking about the right word to complete the description.

"Pathetic." He said the word with disdain.

"After seeing my transformation, even from my previous form, the first thing you thing I would want from you is money? I don't know if I should be amused or insulted."

He sounded like an educated, uptight stiff ass Harvard brat but he wasn't human.

"W-what are you? A-Are y-you d-death?" Alex whispered finally in a shuddering voice.

"Death?" The creature chuckled at her expense. "Oh, you should be so lucky."

Alex found it difficult to breathe. "No woman, I'm far worse than him."

Jason tried again to move from this mysterious hold on him that paralyzed his every muscle in his body except his face.

Alex could not even turn her head. She could not fathom what was going on, why was this thing here; talking with them like this was a normal everyday conversation?

The creature watched her with eyes that were like a hybrid of orbs and black pits.

"I am Ral. You're wondering why I am here?" speaking rhetorically.

Alex only nodded her head. She lost her voice again.

"That's just cruel." He said grinning.

"But you are pathetic humans after all so I am not expecting anything of worth from you." he sighed as if not wanting to do some grueling task.

"I sent something to Earth some time ago, something important to me." The pale light of the moon casted his eyes in the shadows.

"... and it's time to collect." He said slowly pointing a long slim finger at Alex.

"Do you remember now, Alex?" He moved closer to the scared woman. "What your grandmother said about the year of the third?"

Alex jaw dropped and her eyes became impossibly wider, but nothing came out of her mouth.

"Surprised, Alex?"

The girl only nodded and her breath sped up.

"You know what they say Alex," Ral said, "Devils come to collect what's theirs in the shadow of four solar eclipses?"

Alex was trembling with shock so much that, Jason couldn't believe his eyes and ears.

"Are you the D-Devil?" Alex asked in a stuttering voice.

"Not THE devil, but a devil yes. To put it more accurately, a demon, but many a people have call me a devil over the centuries, so I got used to it" He answered casually.

"But, you know Alex, my special pathetic human Alex; I didn't come here to talk, only to collect."

"What are you saying'?" Jason asked. "What are you here to collect?"

"Silence, vermin!" He said in a voice that deafened them in the small bedroom.

"Leave her alone!" Jason yelled with anger and defiance. He was still the man of this house and no demon or devil was going to talk to him in any way he didn't like.

"Who asked you for your opinion?" Ral said irritably, a snarl coming from his lips quelled any possible rebellion from Jason.

"You're lucky you married her because I could have killed her so many times before you two even met."

He stretched out a dirty finger which caused Jason to be pushed away with an invisible force that landed him on the floor between the window and the bed, knocking over the bed side table in the process. Jason could feel that the magical force get stronger as it dragged him up the wall and held him there. It was like the weight of gravity was pushing down on him, pinning and crushing him to the wall.

His eyes were on his wife and the demon and Jason could see how terrified she was. She couldn't even move so Alex started to scream again.

"You will be silent, now." He commanded softly.

Alex sealed her lips immediately and nodded her head as her tears were running down her smooth, cheeks.

Jason wanted to do something, but his whole body was paralyzed. He couldn't move, and his eyes were frozen on Alex and the creature. In the back of his head he wondered if that was on purpose by himself or the demon.

Did this thing want me to watch for something?

"P-Please l-leave us alone," Alex begged.

"Oh, no I don't think I can do that," Ral said indifferently.

Alex was staring in disbelief and stuttered her last sentence. "B-But I"

"B-B-B-But," Ral mocked her, and pointed his finger towards Alex, then moved it quickly towards the wall. That mysterious force raised and pushed the her body, and smashed it against the wall with such power that the sound was like a crashing but instead of the wall breaking, Alex's whole body broke and blood washed the wall and everywhere in the room was covered in red.

"Oh, that was an accident," Ral said amusingly looking at the dead woman's remains. Some of her blood splashing on his face, as he uses his long tongue to lick it off. "No matter, this will make the process easier, anyway."

Jason watch in horror without blinking once. The creature looked at him for a brief moment then took out something from his pocket. Jason wasn't able to see what he was doing as he knelt beside the bed. When Jason rose, the creature said.

"If I had a heart I would erase your memory of all of this but where's the fun in that?" Then he pulled back into the shadows.

In an instant, there was a hole of fire in the floor, bathing the bedroom in an orange light and scorching heat that the creature jumped into and simultaneously, the mysterious force that was restraining Jason from moving vanished.

He burst out in tears.

Jason howled in grief as he stood up and rushed outside. As soon as he ran through the front door, he fell down on his knees leaned his hands against the ground. The tears were running down his cheeks like a stream.

"Alex!" The man's scream combined with weep and howl spread around filling the area. Yet, there was no one who could hear him. This was his fault, he kept thinking. He should have tried to do something to protect her, even if it meant giving his life up for hers, he would do it in a heartbeat.

His howling cries echoed among the nearby trees. They lived so far out of the city because he wanted to be closer to nature and the outdoors lifestyle. He remembered Alex not liking the idea but she did it for him anyway. Witnessing his wife brutal death was an unbearable experience. But not only this, he was also a witness to supernatural activities and he learned that demons were real.

Jason lay in a heap in front of his house, the morning was cool, but he didn't feel it. His heart ached and he wanted to die. Sleep wouldn't come to him because he kept seeing the images in his head.

The demon's face, the screams of Alex, and the moment of her death. His body was in shock, the tragedy shook his whole being. He tried to think, tried to get his bearings of what to do next.

He couldn't go to the police, the worst that they would do is pin the murder of his wife on him, the least was putting him into a strait jacket and shipping him off to the mad house. Slowly, almost like an out of body experience, he went to his house, grabbed some money from behind the clock, took out the car keys from his jacket, and put another jacket on. Then he rushed outside and looked back at the window of his bedroom, only to see that it was covered with blood stains.

He closed his eyes for the moment to see the images again: Alex greeting him previous night, making him supper, then being brutally turned into a pile meat and blood. Jason opened his eyes and got into his car, started the engine and took off. He left the house opened. He didn't call the police, or anyone.

He simply left.

Years went by after the incident with the demon and Jason found himself at the far end of the earth.

The old engine of his jeep roared, he was off somewhere to find something that made some sense to his quest to find Ral and a gateway to Alex. Jason wasn't very good at giving up and the night that thing invaded his home and took the only person in his life that mattered, he decided that he wouldn't rest until he found it and killed it if he had to. He was no soldier, no warrior or anything remotely to that, but he had a purpose and he wasn't about to allow some bastard from hell to make him cower like some yellow belly chicken shit.

He didn't give a damn how long it took, he would find that piece of shit and kill him. Even if he had to go into hell itself. In the time that had passed, Jason took every opportunity to find out more about demons and what they were really. He couldn't go back to his own country since he was wanted for the death of his wife and there was no way they would even throw him in the loony bin now because he ran; and somehow he knew that bastard was somewhere watching him, relishing his pain and sorrow. Sometimes he feels like he's been spied on but maybe it was his own paranoia.

He still didn't know why the demon came after them in the first place. Why did his wife have to die?

Jason took a glance at a small picture attached next to the wheel, the young blonde woman in it- Alex. She was smiling then when they just got married and were on their honeymoon. He sighed and did what he'd learn to do since Alex's death when he thought about her and was about to slip back into the pains of his dark heart. He thought about the demon and what he said that night. There were only pieces of the puzzles, Alex's grandmother, third solar eclipse, collecting.

Unfortunately for him, the old bat died before they got married and her parents were no help when they heard about her death and automatically decided that he was the one responsible for it.

He couldn't say that he blamed them much. He was set up by a freak of nature with super powers; there was not much defense there for him.

Beside him was a large dark skin man covered with tattoos. They were in Kenya, and he was a native. His name was Botan

"Something tells me that here I would find what I am looking for today." Jason said to the large man beside him.

Which is what?" Botan asked with his thick Kenyan accent doubtfully. Though they spoke English, it took a while for him to understand what they were saying.

Botan was a retired doctor and now he hunts for the thrills in one of the best places for hunting in the world.

He has been with Jason for two years now since Jason first arrived on the continent saying that he needed a guide through the African jungles and he was the only one stupid and crazy enough to volunteer, for a price of course. When they started out, there were more of them but who the wild beast of the jungle didn't eat alive, backed out on their own accord.

Jason looked ahead as if he was lost in thought for a moment and he said.

"I don't know yet, Botan. But I do know it's near."

Suddenly Jason spotted something far in the distance in front of him.

"Look! Can you see it Botan?" He shouted with enthusiasm

The tall black man with short curly hair tried squinting his eyes so he could see what his partner was looking at.

"You mean those trees?"

At the same time, Jason pressed the gas harder and the white jeep accelerated. A strong wind cooled the sweat on their faces.

"No, below the trees, those huge rocks," he said eagerly.

"What rocks? I see only sand, no rocks," Botan said doubting the man's mind at this point.

"Are you seeing a mirage right now?" Botan shouted over the roar of the engine.

"No, I'm not," Jason said casually, "I know what I'm seeing."

They stopped the car near the trees and Jason jumped out of it. It was a hunch, a small chance but he would take it.

"The shovel, fast!" Jason demanded and Botan got out and went to the trunk. He opened it and took out a spade.

"Don't tell me that you're going to dig here."

"Of course I am, and you'll help me," Jason replied with a smile.

"I don't get paid enough for this shit." Botan grumbled as he grabs another spade and started to dig in the sand unwillingly.

"The witch doctor from the last village said this was the place, so we dig here." Jason said with delight

Hours passed and now the sun was ready to leave as it sat on the horizon in the west.

"Are you ready to stop and go back to the village?" Botan asked wiping off the sweat off his forehead. After hours of digging they had made an impressive hole in the ground, but had not found anything of significance.

"No, it's here," came the answer. "It must be here! We must be getting close!"

"But can't you see, Jason, that it's no use. There is nothing there. "

"Stop grumbling, we're almost there," Jason said impatiently.

"I tell you, you will find nothing here apart from the sand. Let's go back," Botan insisted.

But just as Jason was about to say something suddenly the spade hit something hard. Both men pause at the sound of the metal clang from the shovel. Jason kneeled and started digging with his hands, getting rid of the sand from the hard object.

"Strange," Botan said looking at his colleague, as he was maniacally brushing off the dirt.

Finally, the sand was removed, revealing something ominous.

Boton looked like he was about to turn pale white. "Oh my God" he mouthed.

Jason wasn't able to say anything. They both stood there in the pit for what seemed like forever, shock tore through the both of them as they looked at what seemed like rotting skeletons melted together on top of something that could only be described as the head of a dragon.

By profession, Jason was an archaeologist and his trained eyes could see that there was something very wrong here. The flesh covering the skeletons were still rotting yet this thing had to be over three thousand years old. But before he could continue with his thoughts, a movement shook him back to reality.

"Did you just see that?" Jason asked a still shocked Botan.

"If you mean if I saw the head move slightly, yes, but I wished that I didn't?"

"Yeah, that." Jason said

"Yeah. I saw it."

The two men bolted from the hole that they dug, which up until now, Botan wasn't sure why and to some extent neither was Jason.

For five years, Jason had been searching for answers to his wife's death and yet for some reason beyond his own logics and sanity, he never really thought that she died that night. He believed in heaven and damn it he wanted to murder a particular demon but that was not what he usually felt when he thought about his wife.

He felt like she was still alive, and when Botan asked about Alex, he always talked like she was still among the living. He had been running for two years but not away because he was framed, it was more like a pull to the answers that he sought.

"You woke me," a snarling growl came from the pit as soon as the men got to the jeep.

The ground under them started to tremble.

"Let's go!" Jason shouted. Botan didn't have to be told twice as he started the engine and the jeep roared to life, he floored the gas and the vehicles tires kicked up a wave of sand as the men drove as fast as they could away.

The ground began to crack as the dragon was now getting up from the ground, his huge wings fan the sands that started a sand storm behind Jason and Botan.

"Oh fucking shit, Jason what the fuck did you do!?" Botan shouted angrily and scared shitless.

Jason couldn't respond as he stared at the dragon the size of two skyscrapers behind them. The beast shook the sand from his massive body and snapped its head in their direction. It was going to come after them, somehow this was all familiar to Jason, like he had seen it in a dream or something.

"You woke me, Jason!" The dragon roared and flapped its wings as it ascended to the air. If there were no words coming up to his brain before, he was definitely mute now.

It was Botan that spoke up first and asked the question in his head.

"How the fuck does that thing know your name?"

Jason just stared at the dragon ascending into the sky blocking out the sun as it did. Fear gripped his tongue and at that moment he was so glad that Boton was the one driving.

"Jason, if we come out of this alive, you are going to tell me everything and then I am going to kill you."

Botan promise as he floored the gas trying to get away from the dragon that was gaining on them.

Somewhere else at that very moment....

Semen streamed from her ears, where one of those brutes shot out on her in heaps intentionally.

A moaned left her mouth miserably as another monster entered her, working his way into her. A few arms held her hands over her head while others powerfully separated her legs. Different limbs wrapped around her body while others squirmed everywhere. Two limbs had mouths, teeth and tongues, which caught her skin, licking, gnawing, and pulling on her areolas. She was lifted off the ground and not able to oppose the evil presence that had her.

"Feels so great," A demon murmured.

This wasn't the first demon inside Alex and she knew it wouldn't be the last. She stopped counting and crying out after the hoard of demons took turns doing with her as they pleased. All she knew was that this deviled spirit was the one pumping into her now and that was all that mattered since she would preferably to have one doing her than numerous devils at the same time .

The demon Ral that took her to this forsaken place chained her up and left her for these things to do as they please with her. Of course it wasn't before he took his pleasure from her first.

"Remember now, pet." He had said when she started screaming for Jason. "You are in my world now, this is hell and you belong to me!"

As he says this he reaches down and cuts into her bare flesh, Alex screams in agony.

"Shhhh Alex, my pet. You must not cry."

"Jason!" Alex cried out none the less and that seemed to anger Ral.

"You call for that coward!?" his human mask that he still wore twisting with rage.

"Why!?"Alex screams

"Because..." Ral says

"Your grandmother, that maggot! In an attempt to save her wretched soul, promised you to me in a blood oath!" he told her in a snarl that hushed her cries to whimpers as she listened to his words. True or false, they were the only explanation for what was going on and why he had invaded her life.

"I am not amused by you calling for your husband and if you try to defy me again; I will cause you suffering beyond your comprehension."

"You belong to me and I will do with you as I see fit." Ral said from behind and then without warning, he pushed into her.

"Stop it!" she cried weakly

She heard Ral laughed as he continued pumping into her from behind frantically.

"You are stubborn." He said through his chuckle and something told her that he wasn't one to go back on his word.

"You will beg for me." Ral snarled in her ear.

"You think because I killed your body that I couldn't harm your soul. Did you believe that you would go to heaven because you were a good little girl?" he thrust up hard and fast while he spoke to her. Growls left his mouth as he did.

"There is so much more I can do you now that your body is dead."

Alex cried out until she could not hear her own voice anymore.

"You called for that coward; you know what I did to him? Do you know what he is doing right now?"

She couldn't think, she could hardly breathe.

"I will have my fill of you and because you disobeyed me, I will have everything that walks in here have a taste of you until you're driven mad. Then I will toss you into the flames of hell and have you relive it seven more times."

Ral had tentacles and he used them to plug her mouth and her other orifices. He did this over and over again for what seem like hours until he roared.

"GGGGGGRRRRR!!" Ral shot his seed into her.

That was some time ago and now here she was unable to wake up from this nightmare.

Five more monsters came at her but she no longer cared.

Initially, she had promised bloody, brutal vengeance to those horny monstrosities. She had cried that she will murder them, cut them up and crush their bones. She trusted that help would come, that she could see Jason again, coming to rescue her but that couldn't happen. Be that as it may, every one of those things was now past and this was her future now until Ral decides to stop it. Innumerable assaults extended her gaps to agonizing extremes.

Her mouth hurt from the consistent sensual caresses she needed to give but Alex didn't dissent as two different evil spirits snatched her hands and did what they wanted with them. The evil presences constrained her muscles and they moved on their own accord.

Jason she thought.

At one point, Botan noticed that they were not going to outrun this dragon. He was still thinking that when the dragon's claws swiped the back of the jeep and the two men went flying. Botan ended up under the jeep as it toppled on top on him after rolling from the force of the dragon's attack. He thought he was going to make it but within a matter of minutes, he was gone.

Jason wasn't so lucky.

He went flying into the sand and his head bashed on a rock and blood ran onto the sands. He was barely conscious enough to see the dragon changed from its massive form to that of a man; a familiar man from five years ago.

"Hello, Jason." Ral said

"You," Jason was barely able to speak.

Ral kicked him and he went flying through the air. As Jason landed he spits out some of his teeth and a mouthful of blood. In an instant Ral was standing beside him again as soon as he hit the ground.

"After all this time, you're still so, this" Ral said with disgust.

"You were the one giving me dreams, sending me visions."

Ral clapped his hands, "very good, but now what?"

Jason wasn't able to see him anymore, his lids were swollen and blinding him from the demon in front of him.

"Will you ask me about Alex, will you tell me that you love her still and how you will give your life to have her back in your arms again? Answer me, vermin!"

Jason laughed and he angered Ral so much that the demon roared and he hit Jason over and over again. How dare a mere human swine laugh at him? Well, he would teach him, he thought with a sneer.

Ral made sure to keep Jason alive just long enough for him to stop and disguise his voice like Alex's, calling for him.

"Alex." Jason cried out weakly.

"I never loved you; you were always just a burden to me." Ral said in Alex's voice.

It was faint but he could see Jason's surprised reaction, he started to sob softly. Ral could smell his pain and it delighted him.

"You should just die." Ral said again making Alex's voice sound like a snarl but Jason was so far gone, he couldn't tell any more.

"I'm so sorry Alex, please forgive me" were his last words.

Ral was a beast of cruelty and pain, a devil that had no sympathy for any one and was cursed to walk the earth feeding on the pain of anyone weak enough to leave the window of opportunity open for him to slip through.

STORY FIVE

YOU CAN RUN, BUT YOU CAN'T HIDE

31.10.2010. 11:11 PM – BRANDON O`CONNOR

"Come out, come out, wherever you are."
Her voice gives me the chills. This isn`t my girlfriend anymore. I don`t know how, but I know it. I guess the fortune teller was right after all. This isn`t a game, it is real, and I am going to die. Because I didn`t believe her. Because I agreed to go to this stupid party. Let`s celebrate Halloween in the cemetery, nothing can go wrong, right? I wish I could go back in time and erase this madness. Or simply wake up, as if from a horrible nightmare. Everything goes quiet for a moment, and I can hear my own heart beating. I`m scared as hell that Amy can hear it, too. I try to hold my breath, but no use. Whoever she is now, or rather whatever she is, will find me anyway. I can only delay the inevitable.

Another gunshot pierces the silence, and I close my eyes in pure terror. I am still alive, so she didn`t shoot me. But that can only mean one thing…

"We can do this for as long as you want. I have time."

It`s Amy again, calling out for me, so that I can end this. I want to, I really do. I wish that nobody else had to die. And I wanted to be a hero. But now that I am facing certain death, I am just a coward. I should have come out of my hiding place behind the gravestone. Preferably before she killed her first victim. But I didn`t. I couldn`t. And now, she is killing them one by one, and nobody can do anything. Except for me. Because it is me who she wants.

There is a thump, and by this time I know the sound too well to ignore it. Another body hits the ground, and I feel sick once more as I glance at Jeremy`s motionless body. My younger brother was the first one she killed. It`s strange how many things have crossed my mind since it happened, and it was only a few minutes ago. Will he come back to haunt me next year? Because his death was my fault, just like all the others. Even if I survive this, which is very unlikely, I will still have to account for that.

"Okay Brandon, I can see that you don`t care about your friends. But what about Amy? You know, I can jump into any of these bodies over here. Let`s see, who shall it be…"

Did she just say that Amy is still alive? Or is this another trick? I don`t care, if there is even a tiny chance that I can save her, I have to try. Even if it means that I have to give up myself. I stand up, turning as quickly as possible. I want to look into her eyes when she kills me. I want that to be the last thing I see before I leave this Earth.

Even if it isn't my girlfriend looking back at me anymore. She looks at me, and I gasp as I realize that there is only darkness where her innocent eyes used to be.

She is covered in blood, and her neck is distorted. I suddenly realize that there is no turning back now, and Amy is gone. I want to cry, I want to scream, asking her what she has done to the love of my life, but I am unable to speak.

All I can do is watch silently and in utter horror as she slowly starts moving closer, aiming her gun at me. For some reason I'm wondering why she needs a gun at all. She is deadly enough even without that. I hear her laugh, and my blood freezes in an instant. The sound is like someone was running a blade along the pavement, one that makes you glance over your shoulders. And alas, I do exactly that, just to wish that I didn't. Jeremy is now standing behind me, as if nothing happened. Although he seems to be alive, I know what I saw. She killed him in front of my own eyes. Parts of his face are missing, ones that were blown off by the bullet. He doesn't seem to care though, he seems to be very much alive. But then, I guess I shouldn't be surprised, considering. I am still shocked though, and a terrible thought doesn't let me give in: why do they need me? Are they going to use my dead body as well? I can't let them do that. At least not without a fight.

"Did you miss me, brother?"

He laughs, and the sound is just as disturbing as hers. I have to keep reminding myself, that this isn't my brother anymore, just like she isn't Amy. And still, who could blame me for not being able to hurt them? Unfortunately, they aren't this careful with me.

31.10.2010. 6:05 PM – AMY FRASER

"All I can see is death."

I glance at Brandon, and I can tell that he is suppressing a chuckle. I must admit, I find this ridiculous myself. Could she be more obvious? Of course, she can see death, it is Halloween after all. The night of the dead, duh. I am about to get up and leave, when the so-called fortune teller grabs my hand. I stop instantly, as her touch is so cold, nearly freezing. This was either a very stupid idea, or it is just another trick of hers. Either way, we can`t stay.

"There is only darkness in your future, and it is starting from tonight."

Okay, I have had enough of this. She is giving me the creeps, and I even had to pay for this. I thought they were supposed to tell you the truth, or at least something positive. I am utterly disappointed, and motion for Brandon to get up, too. He does, and Madame Greta looks at him, then back at me. I guess she finally realized that she won`t get any extra money out of us, so she lets go of my hand. She is still shaking her head when we leave the tent.

For some reason, I feel much better straight away, and there is no sign of my previous uneasiness. I glance back over my shoulder, and her tent looks like a huge monster in the dark. A shudder runs through me, and for the first time I wonder what she meant. Could she have been genuinely concerned?

"What was that all about?"

I look at Brandon, and he smiles at me, so I shrug my shoulders.

"Another scam artist, I guess. It's a good job we only paid for one of us, heh?"
I try to make a joke of it, but the pit in my stomach returns. I wouldn't tell him though, because I can't even explain what I feel or where it is coming from. It might just be my paranoia talking. I want to know my future, but I convinced myself that darkness isn't the only thing that's in it. True, I have never been a saint, but still, it would be a bit harsh to say that all there is is darkness and death. She could have seen my past, but not my future, that's for sure.
"Earth to Amy, what are you thinking about, babe?"
Brandon's voice brings me back from memory lane, and I couldn't be more glad that he is here with me. He has been trying so hard to convince me that everything would be OK. Ever since…
"It's nothing, I just think that this stupid woman got under my skin."
His look is even more concerned now, and I know that I shouldn't have said this. He is thinking the same as I am. What if the past repeats itself?
"It wasn't your fault, you know that, right?"
He pulls me close, caressing my hair, and I feel the urge to let it all go. But I can't afford to do that. I have been strong since the accident, and this isn't going to be the time when I lose it. If it wasn't for me, my sister would still be alive. And I have to live with that. I was the one who drove the car, and I was drunk. There are no excuses, nothing to ease my pain. And I don't deserve that anyway. I break free from Brandon's embrace, and look into his eyes once more as I say:
"Don't worry, I'm fine. Now let's go and pick out our costumes for tonight."

His cheeky smile returns and he nods in agreement. I feel a little bit better, or rather I force myself to feel better and we walk up to the fancy-dress shop.

31.10.2010. 11:29 PM – BRANDON O`CONNOR

I have no idea what they want. I thought that they would kill me by this time, but all they do is laugh. Or is this their way of driving me crazy, so that I would take my own life? What would they gain from that? They like to watch? They make my skin crawl with that sound. I look at Jeremy again, and his eyes are full of madness. My heart breaks as I remember how scared he was of this night. He used to tell me when we were little that monsters were real. He would tell me that something pulled on his leg while he was asleep, or that there was a dark figure in the room. I wish I would have listened to him that time, but I was so certain that nothing of that sort existed. I was wrong.

Now that I am laying on the cool marble, waiting for them to strike, all I can think of is where I went wrong. Was it when I told him that everything would be okay? How could I have known? I try to move, but once again I realize that there is no point. Whatever they are planning to do with me, I am theirs now. Jeremy takes a step closer, and there is something wicked about his expression. I can`t explain why, but it seems like he is enjoying this. He isn`t your brother. Jeremy is gone.

"Oh, actually, he is right here, screaming inside. He is begging me to let you go. Oh, well, never mind."

Did he actually know what I was thinking? This is impossible. And what did he just say about Jeremy? Why are they playing tricks with me? Why give me hope that both of them are still there deep inside, if I have no chance of freeing them?

"So that they can watch as we tear you apart. Let the fun begin, shall we?"

And with that they both start laughing again, slowly walking towards me, both holding a knife. I close my eyes, hoping that I can at least ease my suffering. Of course, it doesn`t work. I can keep my composure when they first cut into my sensitive flesh, but after the third time I hiss. Their blade doesn`t reach deep, just enough so that it gives me agonizing pain. They haven`t finished with me yet, but I just want to know why.

"Oh, darling, that`s very simple."

I open my eyes, and Amy (or what`s left of her) is staring at me. People say that one`s eyes are the reflection of one`s soul, and I don`t even dare believe this is true, because where once I saw love and Amy`s pure soul, there is only darkness now. A black hole that is ready to consume me and anyone who stands in its way. She smiles at me, while her long fingers trace a line along my jaw. Her touch is nearly tender, and for a second my hope returns, just to be crashed by her evil laughter a moment later. She pulls away, and adds while turning around:

"You are the only one who didn`t want to bring me back. So, for that, you are going to suffer."

Although my mind is numb, I recall the moment when Jeremy asked me if I would help him bring Lucy back. Could this be...?

"Now that you have guessed who is in Amy's body, the only thing left is to figure out who I am. This is going to be so much fun."

And with that he slices a bit off my right palm, making me cry out in pain. He seems to be satisfied, but it's hard to tell. My whole body is aching, and I feel nauseated. I haven't lost too much blood yet, but I can already feel the exhaustion that eventually comes with it all. I have seen this many times, having driven an ambulance for nearly ten years. But now that it is happening to me, I can't think of any of the comforting words that I used to tell those who were about to die. I suddenly realize that nothing would be good enough. But at least I was there for them, and I am going to die alone. My brother and girlfriend are gone, and there are so many things I wanted to tell them. But now it is too late. I close my eyes once more, ready to give in to the temptation of blissful obliviousness.

31.10.2010. 7:38 PM – AMY FRASER

"You look ridiculous in that."

Brandon is laughing at me now, and as I look at my reflection, I feel like doing the same. These costumes are just not the same anymore.

I thought that the whole point of Halloween was to scare people, and yet looking at these idiotic masks makes me laugh instead.

Or maybe our perception changed, and what used to terrify us doesn`t scare us anymore. I don`t know, but surely I don`t look like an evil witch in this fluffy purple and black outfit. I decide to change into a more daunting vampire one. At least that has the teeth and fake blood to go with it.

"You can`t complain yourself."

I say laughing, realizing that Brandon is dressed as a giant pig. What does that have to do with spirits and the supernatural? He takes his mask off, grinning at me like an idiot.

"Don`t worry babe, there are plenty of others here. How about Frankenstein?"

And he mimics the movements of the creature, looking like a complete idiot. He has always managed to make me smile, and somehow forget what happened. But I can`t think about that now. Tonight is for celebration.

"Look what I found!"

I hear Jeremy shout at us, and I shudder at the sudden sound. Brandon is looking at me with the same worried expression as before, but I shrug it off, saying that I am a bit more jumpy than usual, that`s all. I turn around, so that I can look at what he got as well, but my eyes are quickly drawn to something else. I believe the horror is reflected on my face, as Jeremy places a hand on my shoulder, in an attempt to calm me down.

"Are you alright, Amy?"

I can hear their question that comes in unison, but in spirit I am far away. I simply can`t take my eyes off the apparition. This can`t be possible.

I want to shout or scream, or at least say something, but I am shocked and dumbfounded. Lucy is standing outside of the shop, staring at me with eyes full of anger and revenge. Her clothes are torn, and her features are a bit grey, but I could swear that it is my sister. I feel cold all of a sudden, and a myriad of emotions rush through me, all at the same time. But most of all I`m scared. She raises a bony finger, and point's right at me.

You are going to be next.

It`s as if I heard her voice, but it must have been a trick of my mind, as her lips don`t move. In fact, all of this might just be my imagination. I must have taken this whole celebration way too seriously. Or this could be a bad dream. Yes, and then when I wake up, she will be gone.

"Amy, what do you see?"

I can hear Brandon`s voice again, and I can feel that he is gently shaking me. I try to look at him, I do. But I can`t. It`s as if I was under a spell or paralyzed. I close my eyes for a second, hoping that when I open them again, she would be gone. I just can`t take this, it is too much. I want to let go of my fear, my anger, and my frustration. But most of all, I need to release the guilt, otherwise it will consume me. Suddenly the fortune teller`s words come to my mind: There is only darkness in your future, and it is starting from tonight. She was wrong. It started two years ago, when I killed my sister. I force myself to look up, and I am shocked and relieved at the same time, because she is gone. I let out a nervous breath, and I realize that I am shaking all over.

I am finally able to turn towards Brandon and Jeremy, and both of them are scared for me. Do they feel pity, too? That`s the least thing I need right now. They surely think that I am a damaged girl, not worth having in their lives. Where the hell are these thoughts coming from? I shake my head, trying to shake the thoughts as well, but I can`t stop feeling miserable.

"Did you see her?"

I hear myself ask, and I wish that I didn`t. I can`t take it back now. I watch intently as Brandon narrows his eyes and the two brothers exchange a strange look. Here we go again.

"See who, Amy? There wasn`t anyone outside."

My heart starts pounding as his words sink in. I am furious now, how could they do this to me?

"What kind of sick joke are you playing? Is this funny to you? Well, guess what. Halloween or not, I am not putting up with this."

I try to run out of the shop, because I can feel tears starting to run down my cheek. Jeremy grabs my arm and pulls me back, forcing me to face him.

"Listen, Amy. Whatever or whoever you saw was just an illusion. There was nobody there, and you know that we wouldn`t lie about this. Isn`t it, Brandon?"

I look at my boyfriend, and he nods reassuringly. I wipe away a tear, and although I have no idea what just happened, I decide that there is no point in me getting all worked up about this.

"Okay, I believe you. Let`s go to this stupid party."

Although I guess we all wish we could spend the night home instead.

31.10.2010. 9:32 PM – BRANDON O`CONNOR

I am worried about Amy. She hasn`t been herself today. Although I know that this is the anniversary of Lucy`s death, not to mention Halloween, which is creepy enough in itself, still, she is different. Lucy died two years ago, and time is supposed to heal wounds, not reopen them with so much force. The look on her face earlier was pure horror, and I wish I could see what she saw. Maybe then I would be able to help. I am pretty sure that even if there was something, it was a silly prank from one of the guys at the party. And yet, she is still so shaken up. She has been drinking since we got here, which is very unlike her. Normally she would be the one who would take me and my brother home. But not tonight. What could be so horrible that she feels the need to forget it like this?

"Ready for another round?"
She asks seductively, obviously not referring to the alcohol. I need to get her home safe.
"Look, Amy, I think you have had enough. Let me drive you home."
She shakes her head, and I can spot fear in her eyes again. Is she this scared of being alone?
"Nah, thanks, but I would rather stay. I love it here."

She swings her paper cup around, as if we were in some posh ballroom. A shiver runs through me as the wind blows through the holes in my clothes. I quickly look around, and the cemetery is full of celebrating people. It is hard to tell who is who, and I can`t see Jeremy anywhere. Part of me is angry with him, as he has a tendency of scaring innocent kids, and I guess this time isn`t different, either. But another part of me is worried, because he has been gone for ages. I know that these are just costumes, but still, people can hear about so many crimes committed on this day. Amy is clinging to my arm, so I decide to distract her:

"Have you seen Jeremy?"

She seems confused for a second, trying to sober up, and then nods enthusiastically:

"Oh, yes, he was going towards the crypt about an hour ago. Why?"

The crypt? Great, as if I didn`t have enough problems already. I let out an exasperated sigh, reassuring her that everything is fine, I will just go and get my brother here, so we can all go home.

"You are joking, right? Why do you always have to ruin someone else`s fun?"

What? Is she serious? I find it difficult to convince myself that she is just drunk and doesn`t know what she is talking about, but I manage to remain calm when I reply:

"I`m sorry hon, I will make up for it later."

This normally works, but not this time. She shakes her head, turning around.

"Where do you think you are going?"

I ask in shear desperation, but she shoots me a murderous look and I know better than to argue with her.

"Do not follow me, or I will never talk to you again."

And with that she disappears into the darkness of the night. For a moment, I wonder whether I should go after her despite the threat, but decide to give her a few minutes` advantage.

31.10.2010. 9:40 PM – AMY FRASER

I know that I was a bit harsh and Brandon didn`t deserve the way I spoke to him. I am not half as drunk as he thinks I am. I feel terrible for pretending that I am wasted, just because I don`t want to talk about what happened. This doesn`t mean that I don`t think about it though. Whatever I saw back in the shop, was the most real thing I ever experienced. It was as if the air became freezing and all the lights went out. All I could see was my dead sister. What sort of sick joke is this? She has been dead for two years now, and yet whenever I close my eyes, the scene appears in front of my mind`s eyes every single time. I can`t shake it, it`s as if she was here with me. But not supporting me, no. Nurturing my self-blame and guilt. I know that I am responsible for what happened, but I didn`t think this would be possible.

My feet get caught up in something, and it takes all my strength to maintain my balance. I am desperate to divert my thoughts, so I try to focus on finding Jeremy instead. I wonder why he disappeared all of a sudden, but then I guess he misses her as much as I do. I still remember when we were crying on each other`s shoulders after she died. He loved her, but until then I didn`t know just how much. Poor Jeremy, he is only a kid, and already he lost so much. And that`s another reason why I have to find him.

I reach the crypt, and I find the door wide open, which is strange, considering that the caretaker normally locks it when he leaves. But then again, it might as well be an attraction for the night. I take a step closer, but my heart skips a beat as I hear a noise behind me. I start to panic, and I have to close my eyes in order to keep my composure. I ask in a quivering voice:

"Who is there?"

But there is no answer. I gulp more loudly than I want to, forcing myself to open my eyes and turn around, terrified of what I might see. And my worst fears come true as Lucy is standing in front of me, or rather the apparition from before. I want to run, but once again I am paralyzed.

"What do you want from me?"

I shout at her, but she still doesn`t answer. She takes a step towards me, and I involuntarily take a step back. No, this can`t be happening. Amy, wake up! This is a bloody nightmare. Her skin starts to fade off, and by the time she reaches me, her features are gone. She touches me with her bony finger, and I try to scream, but my voice is just a tiny whisper. Her fingers are cold, and yet their touch burns like hell. I gather all my courage and break free, turn around and run inside the crypt. As soon as I close the doors behind me, I let out the breath I have been holding in.

I look around, trying to get used to the lack of light, when Jeremy`s voice breaks the silence:

"What are you doing here, Amy?"

I try to figure out where he is, but it seems like the sound is coming from everywhere. And then I spot a tiny candle in the distance, and decide to go closer to see what`s happening.

Jeremy is sitting on the floor, and there is something shiny in front of him. He slowly stands up, and I can see what it is: a knife. He is surrounded by candles and skulls. I look at him, not sure what this whole thing is about. I feel uneasy again, but this time it is different. There is just something in his eyes that`s not right. As if something was different now, but what?

"What is this, Jeremy?"

I motion towards the items, and he follows the movement of my hand with his eyes. A small smile appears on his lips, and it is replaced by a laughter that makes me even queasier. "Oh, that. Well, you weren`t supposed to see that. But now that you have, let me tell you a little secret."

He kneels down, places his palms on both of his knees, then closes his eyes and asks me to do the same. I am hesitating, but after a few seconds I decide that no matter how weird this looks, he must have a rational explanation. He is Brandon`s brother, after all. I do as he asked, and as I close my eyes, I can see the same picture again. My sister.

"Jeremy, I can`t take this anymore."

I can feel his soothing hand on my shoulder when he says:

"I know, love, I know. But don`t worry, I am going to bring her back. And you are going to help me."

I want to ask him what the hell he means, but it is too late. A sharp pain courses through my entire body, forcing me to open my eyes. Jeremy places his hand in front of my mouth, stabbing me with the other one more time. Why is he doing this? I can feel my mind go numb, and my eyes are closing again. This time for ever, I`m sure.

31.10.2010. 10:21 PM – BRANDON O`CONNOR

I glance at my watch. I have waited enough, and they aren`t back. I am going after her, and she can thank me later for it. There is a tap on my shoulder, and I turn around, ready for a fight, when I find myself staring into Amy`s eyes. Although they seem to be a bit different now. For some reason, she is giving me the creeps. What the hell is wrong with me? She is my girlfriend, for God`s sake. It seems like this nonsense has gotten to me as well. She smiles at me, grabbing my hand, and I freeze. Her touch is cold, and not the way it would be when you are outside in winter, but in a completely different way. She leans close, and I am about to ask about Jeremy, when she whispers into my ear:

"Oh, love, aren`t you happy to see me again?"

Her voice… This isn`t real, she is playing some kind of trick on me, I`m sure. I didn`t even know how good an actress she was, but she would definitely deserve an Oscar for this performance.

"Of course I am. Where is Jeremy?"

She looks into my eyes once more, and this time I could swear I see the light go out. All there is left is darkness.

"Don`t worry about him, darling. He isn`t going to suffer anymore. I have missed you. So, what is it going to be? Shall we play a little game?"

01.11.2010. 6:21 AM – BRANDON O`CONNOR

It takes me a few minutes (or maybe hours, I wouldn`t be able to tell) to take in my surroundings. The events of last night slowly start to come back to me. Amy and Jeremy dying, their unconscious bodies inhabited by those entities or whatever they were. The pain, the fear, the blood. I have no idea why they didn`t finish what they started, but somehow I am still alive. Maybe this was their plan all along. They wanted to make me suffer. Because I didn`t want to bring Lucy back. And now I am left alone, because she has taken the two people I loved the most.

I look around, and they are gone. Completely disappeared. I have no idea what happened, or where they went, but I know that they wanted to punish me. And I deserve it. So many people died because of me, but the ones I care about I condemned to a fate way worse than death. I know that this isn`t over, nor is my punishment. I try to stand up, but my feet fail me. I think I have a broken rib or two as well. For a moment, I think that I`m not going to survive this, but then I remember that it wouldn`t be as cruel as if they let me live.

I can hear sirens in the background. So, they made sure that I would be saved. So that they can come back and haunt me. A shiver runs through me, and as I glance around, trying to assess the amount of blood I lost, I find a note sticking out of my pocket. I take it out with shaking hands, reading the handwritten lines over and over again, until all my hope disappears:

Wait for me, love, I won`t be long. I will return this time next year. Don`t forget the fun we had tonight, I sure won`t. oh, and by the way, just so you know: Amy and Jeremy are still with me, and until my return, I am going to have some fun with them, just to keep me entertained. Relax, I am not going to hurt them. Well, not that much, that is. Farewell, Brandon, take care of yourself.

P.S.: I always loved you, but you chose my sister. Oh, well, now you know. I wish you wanted to bring me back, I do. But we can still be together forever. As a family.

Love,

Lucy

STORY SIX

THE BUNKER

"Huhh huhh huhh …"

The ceiling came into focus, then out again. This happened in quick succession. His vision returned to him in waves, in rhythm with the blood he felt flowing through his temples. He could feel the dust matted to his skin by his own sweat. He tried focusing on the spots of dried paint, peeling from the ceiling. The smell of rotting flesh suddenly hit him particularly hard as he tried to shift his position. As he attempted to sit up, pain shot through his neck and down his back. He decided to remain stationary for the moment, patting his body with gloved hands, trying to access his injuries. The solid plate carrier held strong, and he looked to his hands and was relieved not to see any blood. He continued to pat himself down, reaching as far toward his legs as he could. Examining his hands once more, another sigh of relief…no blood. He then looked toward his feet, hoping not to see any signs of a critical injury.

His legs were intact, and he clicked the toes of his combat boots together to confirm he still had movement in his legs. From what he could see, he appeared all right, still in once piece. But it became apparent he had taken some sort of head injury. His forehead throbbed and there was still a bit of pain emanating from his neck. He reached for the back of his head and then examined his brown glove. There was some blood, but not thick. At least he had narrowed down the location of his injury.

The soldier laid there, trying to put some kind of image together in his scattered mind, reaching for any recent memories to help him understand his current situation. There were many mixed images in his head, but none he could interpret. His brain seemed to have fuddled up, as if he was trying to listen to too many radio stations at once. He tried to concentrate on just one of the memories, but the more he tried the more they blurred together... just like sand. The soldier's frustration began to mount, as he lay there in pain, overcome with confusion.

His vision was beginning to improve as the throbbing pain in his head subsided. He looked to his left and saw the sharpening image of a window. Somehow it disturbed him, even in the sub consciousness of his scattered mind. He began to realize that someone had tried to cover the window with wooden planks and blockade it with furniture in a rather haphazard way. There were obviously in a desperate rush. There was just enough to cover the entrance. As he tried to focus his vision, the stress on his eyes began forcing his swollen lids shut.

Suddenly, he heard a nearby voice calling out. He could barely hear it above the loud ringing in his ears. He shot up quickly to see who else was in the room with him, but another sharp pain jolted through his body as result of his quick movement. He was sitting up now, and despite the pain, he had no intention of laying back down. He swayed sideways and forced his eyes to reopen as he struggled to get his head to stop spinning. The dark room was slightly lit by the last, escaping rays of the setting sun. He could see a number of oddly placed chairs, tables, broken lamps and candles scattered around the room. He winced as he made his way to his hands and knees, breathing heavily and grunting repeatedly as he fought the pain. He cautiously prepared to post himself onto one foot when he was interrupted yet again by another muffled yell. Filled with a sense of urgency, the soldier stood up to his feet, and paused for a moment until the room stopped spinning. He staggered toward the doorway and out of the room, into a dark hallway. There was barely enough light for him to see the objects scattered across the floor. Shards of glass popped and scraped the floor underneath his boots, as he felt his way down the hall toward the sound of the voice, now yelling "help" over and over. The hall was way cooler than the room he was in, and the thick air was filled with a dank odor that terrorized his sense of smell. The odor was putrid, and so strong that he could actually taste it.

He recognized it as the smell of decomposing flesh, as it tugged at his gag reflex. As he forced his way through the hallway and thick, ripe odor, he began to struggle within his own mind as to why he recognized this smell immediately, and why he was so certain it was decomposition. Orange light danced across his face as he passed several small windows that were boarded up, making his way toward the calls for help. He could see the sun was quickly setting as the light shining through the spaces between the planks became less and less. As he got closer to the source of the desperate calls, a fog began to fill the hallway. This confused him as he pushed his way forward, losing even more visibility with every step he took.

Just as he was about to call out to the voice, he felt something organic through his boot.

"Watch it asshole", grunted a low voice through the darkness.

The confused soldier looked down and squinted his eyes to get a better view of the person he had stumbled upon through the confusion of darkness. Suddenly, a dim red light produced from a flashlight illuminated himself and the figure holding it. The soldier could now see this man was wearing an identical uniform. Him sitting on the floor with his back against the hallway wall, looking up at the man who had just walked blindly into him.

"Miller, stop standing there and help me damn it!" the man exclaimed.

The soldier immediately recognized this to be his own name.

"Yeah, it's me Miller," he answered with slight hesitance.

"No shit it's you numb nuts, now help me!" the other soldier continued, grunting through obvious pain.

"I got hit back there, you've got to patch me up, man. This shit hurts bad!"

Although Miller could not associate a name with the man's face, Miller was sure he knew him. "Look," the soldier said, trembling as he turned the flashlight toward himself. He was holding the light in his left hand while clutching his left shoulder with his right hand. An abundance of liquid covered the man's hand and soaked his sleeve around it as he looked up, gritting his teeth together in obvious pain. It was obvious he was bleeding.

"Miller," the man repeated, "I'm a bit fucked up, man. This friggin hurts!"

Miller was just as confused as he was concerned for the injured soldier at his feet. He knelt down on one knee as if to examine the man, but he still had no idea who he was. He could see several tears throughout the man's uniform, but not very much blood.

Miller placed his hands on the man and began patting him down gently, examining him for more wounds. "Who …?" He started to ask, but was interrupted with a sharp growl of pain from the man the moment Miller touched his left arm. The man began squirming and kicking his legs. He grunted loudly through his clinched teeth, his eyes shut tightly.

"Morphine!" the soldier grunted. "C'mon Doc, gimme some!"

Miller looked down at his plate carrier, examining his kit for some sign of a med-kit. He quickly grabbed his IFAK, but was dismayed once he felt it was completely empty. "How the fuck…" he mumbled with confusion.

"C'mon Doc, I need it now!" the wounded soldier grunted sharply through his teeth.

"I don't have any!" Miller exclaimed, his voiced filled with panic.

With those words, the wounded soldier lifted his left arm with great effort, not removing his good hand from his bleeding wound. "There", he blurted.

Looking in the direction illuminated by red light, miller saw a large tactical bag with a medical cross on the center pouch facing him. Miller scrambled for the pack, despite his own pain. The bag was surrounded by empty wrappers, and several bloody bandages. Snatching up the bag, Miller's heart sank when the main pouch flapped right open. The bag was completely unzipped and felt light as a feather in his hand.

Miller then placed the bag between the wounded soldier's legs. "Point it there", Miller ordered. The bag was filled with red light as Miller pummeled through each pouch thoroughly, sifting through clamps and catheters.

"Here!" Miller exclaimed with relief as he finally grasped a single morphine auto-injector.

"Hurry," the man grunted.

Miller injected the Soldier and within moments, the soldier began to breathe with steady relief. He relaxed his jaw and closed his eyes, almost as if being filled with a sudden calm.

Miller examined the man's face. He was familiar, very familiar. Miller was almost certain he knew him. He saw a name tape on the soldier's plate carrier. "Wentworth", it read.

"Wentworth," Miller stated the moment the bleeding soldier seemed to getting his wits about him. "I got to sling and bandage your arm, but I need more light. There are some candles in the room I was in. I'm going to grab them and come right back. Gimme the light so I can get there and back quickly."

Wentworth responded with a subtle smile, "take your time Doc", and placed the light in Miller's hand. Miller did exactly as he planned, and was back with candle within minutes. Wentworth was already waiting with a cigarette lighter in his hand. "75th" was engraved into it.

The two soldiers were now surrounded by the light of five candles. Miller had all the light he needed to properly bandage and sling Wentworth's arm. With the few remaining bandages from the bag he found on the floor, Miller went to work.

"You're lucky, you know why?" Miller said sternly as he worked on the soldier's wound. "The bullet passed right through. From what I can tell it didn't break apart. Looks like it was 5.56 though. How did you get shot?"

Wentworth nodded his head and licked his lips slowly. "Yeah, man. It was Johannson. He was providing cover fire with Lee as I stuffed you into the truck. I yelled to him to jump in the back, but those fuckers swarmed him from every side. It must have been a reflex shot, he went down shooting and I got hit." Then he paused for moment, his eyes becoming glassy. "I watched as they tore into him," his voice cracked, trying to fight back a sudden rush of grief. I can still hear him screaming, man. Fuck, man. Fuck!"

Miller paused from bandaging the wound, obviously confused by Wentworth's description of events. "Soooo, they engaged Johannson but didn't shoot at us?"

"They weren't shooting at dick, Miller, they fucking swarmed him and ripped him apart," Wentworth raised his voice, clearly annoyed with Miller's line of questioning. "They literally swarmed him like locusts and tore into him with their hands and their fucking teeth."

Miller stared into Wentworth's eyes, his face twisted with confusion. "They...ate Johannson?"

"Ugghhh," Wentworth grunted as he rolled the back of his head to the wall, banging it multiple times with frustration. "Yes, Doc. They fucking ate him, right in front of me! Fuck!"

Miller was stunned by what he was hearing. He began to think that perhaps Wentworth had lost more blood than he realized. Or perhaps the morphine was affecting the wounded soldier's mind. Maybe he had taken a head injury. Whatever the cause, Wentworth was clearly delirious. Miller needed to try a new angle in order to figure out their current situation.

"Okay, man, we are both banged up," Miller said as he continued to finish bandaging Wentworth's shoulder. "I know the situation seems pretty FUBAR right now, but we gotta keep it together if we want to make it through whatever is going one. We gotta link up with the rest of the squad and get back to the FOB. Where are the others? None of them EXFILed with us?"

Wentworth opened his eyes and looked directly into Millers with an expression so Grim, Miller's heart began to sink with anxiety over what Wentworth would say next. "There was no EXFIL. Listen to me very carefully", he said as he grabbed the collar of Miller's uniform top, pulling him within a few inches of his face, "we are all that's left. You and me, Doc. Everyone else is dead."

A cold chill shot through Miller's body, immediately followed by a sick feeling in his stomach. He couldn't believe what he was hearing. Wentworth continued staring directly into Miller's eyes blankly for another moment, then he smiled and rolled his head back against the wall.

"You don't remember a damn thing, do you?" he asked, smirking. "Shit, this is getting better by the minute."

"Just tell me what happened, man. Where the fuck are we? What the hell happened to the rest of the platoon?" Miller replied impatiently, frustration and anger coursing through his veins.

Wentworth blinked a few times before answering, "By the time we realized what was happening, we got swarmed by them."

"Them? Who the fuck is them, Wentworth!?" Miller interrupted, clearly losing his patience as his confusion continued to mount. "Who hit us!?"

Wentworth stared blankly into Miller's eyes for several seconds. "The dead", he finally replied, flatly and without blinking. "Fucking corpses, man."

Miller just stared at the man. He swallowed hard, searching for words to respond to Wentworth's words. He knew this was not a side effect from the drugs he had used to numb his fellow soldier's gunshot wound. He didn't believe blood loss was the cause either. At this point, Miller was convinced Wentworth had lost it. Whatever actually happened was so traumatic, that it broke Wentworth's mind. Perhaps he actually did see their platoon mates die, and it was too much for him to handle. Miller swallowed hard again, and prepared his next line of questions carefully. He wanted to see exactly how far his fellow soldier had descended into madness.

"Okay, if we were attacked by corpses, how did I get knocked out? Did they knock me out?" he asked, careful not to make it obvious he was questioning the soldier's sanity.

Wentworth dropped his eyes to the floor, his mouth open as if he was contemplating how he would replay. "Nah Doc, Johannson knocked you out," he finally answered, hesitantly. "He saved your life in the process."

Miller frowned with confusion. "Why did Johannson attack me?"

"He didn't attack you," Wentworth replied, looking back into Miller's eyes. "You were going ape shit. Jackson and Lee got swarmed just a few yards from us. They were screaming as those things tore into them. I and Johannson knew there was nothing we could do to help them, but you started running toward them like you actually thought you could save them.

I grabbed you and tried to pull you away. You were yelling at me to let go, but your screams only put their attention back on us. Those things had already cut us off from the ARMRAPs. The only way out was a Haji technical, the shitty S10 I boosted to get us here. I was trying to pull you to the truck, but you were fighting me, trying to get to Jackson and Lee. They were already dead at that point, but you were hysterical, man. Johannson hit you with a butt strike to the back of your head to get you to stop. I guess with all the adrenaline, he hit you too hard and you went out. I threw you into the bed of the truck and jumped into the driver's seat. Anyway, those things swarmed Johannson before he could get clear. That's when he discharged his weapon into my shoulder, then I floored it. I heard some gunfire as we were driving off, but I'm sure it was Johannson's reflex. I thought I might eventually pass out, so I drove as fast as I could until we were eventually out of the city, away from the hoards. I haven't seen anyone since. The radio's been silent too. We're all that's left, Doc".

Miller remained silent for several moments. He was actually stunned by Wentworth's detailed explanation of events. Of course what he was saying was crazy, but he seemed fully coherent. "So, where are we?" he asked plainly.

Wentworth closed his eyes and leaned his head against the wall again. "Man, I don't know. I just tossed your ass in the truck, and drove as far away from that fuckery as the gas tank would take us. Shitty part is, we didn't make it that far. This bunker is just maybe a mile from where shit went down. The truck got peppered during the initial contact with Hadji, before those things showed up. Most the gas had already leaked through the holes before we boosted it. I saw this bunker from the road in the distance and figured we were better off in here than stranded with no cover further down the road. There aren't as many of them on the road as in the town, but we are still in danger."

Miller dropped his eyes, carefully thinking of his response. "Okay," he started, "well I'm back on my feet now and I'm pretty sure you can walk too. Maybe we can find a vehicle outside and make our way to the FOB."

"Slow down, Doc," Wentworth chuckled. "Those fuckers may be on foot, but they are fast. They started showing up about 20 minutes ago. Plus they know we're here. This place is pretty much surrounded by a few dozen of those things. I barely had enough time to fix the blockades."

"Fix them?" Miller replied, clearly perplexed.

"Yeah, man", Wentworth nodded his head. "Somebody got here before us and closed off the windows and most of the doors. The main entrance was the only one that we could access on the way in. I guess whoever was here didn't feel that safe. They must have split moments before we got here. And if there was a vehicle outside, they used it to make their getaway."

Miller sat quietly for a moment. What he was hearing was madness, but Wentworth was speaking so matter of factly, without any hesitation.

"So you're telling me that if I look out a window, I will see zombies walking around right outside?" Spencer said, pointing to boarded up window just left of the main entrance down the hall from them.

"No, that window's boarded up completely, but there's a small viewing porthole in the main door. You can see them through that," Wentworth said looking directly into Miller's eyes, no expression on his face. "Careful, they know we are in here. They just haven't figured out how to get in. Leave that door closed."

Without saying a word, Miller stood up and quickly headed to the door. There was a thick chain wrapped around the large handles, but the lock was missing. The door was made of heavy metal and very robust. There were several heavy duty hinges holding it to a thick steel door frame. Four separate locks were spaced a few inches from one another, each one alone capable of withstanding small arms fire. In the center, there was a small viewing porthole, just about eye level. It was in the shape of a rectangle, five inches wide and three inches high. It was obviously made of thick ballistic glass, several inches thick. It was obvious to Miller that nothing was coming through that door unless it was invited in. Between that, and the thick concrete walls that comprised the structure of the building and all its room's, a slight bit of ease lifted within Miller.

He approached the robust door cautiously not knowing what to expect to see on the other side. He was half expecting to see nothing but an empty lot, but was preparing in his mind to see some kind of armed, hostile presence. He put his face up to the door and looked through the narrow porthole. What he saw cut his breath in half.

A soldier, wearing a US Army uniform, was standing just a few yards away on the other side of the door. His back was turned to Miller, but blood was matted to the back of his body armor and ballistic helmet. The uniform was torn in many places, open flesh visible through the holes in the fabric. Furthermore, the soldier was missing his right arm at the elbow, with the right side of the uniform covered in blood below the amputation, dripping from the rib cage all the way down to his boot ankle.

"Oh my God!" Miller blurted as he grasped the top most latch with both hands, fumbling to unlock it quickly.

"Doc, don't you open that door!" Wentworth's stern voice echoed down the hall.

Miller ignored him, his priority was to pull that badly injured soldier into the bunker and treat his wounds. After all, miller was a combat life saver. Saving lives was his primary role in the battlefield. Great anger filled Miller as he imagined this poor soldier standing outside for God only knows how long, desperately in need of medical attention. Wentworth's delusions may very well cost this soldier his life in the long wrong. Miller looked up as he grasped the final latch to make sure the soldier wasn't wandering away or had passed out. He froze once he regained sight of the soldier.

The soldier was now standing just a few feet from the door, facing the direction of the noise made by Miller's fumbling of the latches. Miller's bottom lip began to quiver as he witnessed the extent of the soldier's grave injuries.

His entire abdomen and chest cavity had been ripped away, exposing bone and even what remained of the heart. The withered remains of what was left of his intestine were hanging freely from the cavity that used to be the soldier's stomach. The damage extended up into the soldier's face. The flesh from the chin to the tip of his nose had been torn away, exposing bone and teeth. Despite all of this, one thing stood out in particular to Miller. The blood was clearly dried, and the exposed inner tissue appeared leathery, as if the wounds were inflicted days ago. The soldiers yellow eyes and grey/purple skin were all signs of massive amounts of blood loss. Fatal amounts.

Miller knew there was absolutely no way a human could survive such injuries without immediate medical treatment, and even then survival would be a long shot. "How in the hell is this guy even standing, let alone alive?" Miller asked himself in astonishment. Miller focused his eyes like an eagle on the mangled flesh, trying to get some sort of idea of what caused the trauma. Yet what remained of the soldier's flesh bore no signs of powder burns or shrapnel. The wounds were jagged, so there was no reason to presume the flesh was cut from his body by a blade or any other conventional tool. In fact, the wounds were very jagged, and surrounded by smaller oval shaped abrasions and gauges. Miller focused his eyes through the small opening just inches in front of his face. He was nearly pressing his forehead against the door trying to get a closer look.

"What the fuck?" he whispered to himself out loud. "Those are...bite marks. Fucking teeth." Miller felt his body go numb. He had a sick feeling come over him in an instant. "No, no fucking way," he said shaking his head. "They ate him? ", he choked.

Then Miller suddenly came to an even more puzzling realization. "H-he's still standing..." he stammered.

"Standing, but not alive," Wentworth's voice said flatly from only a few feet away.

Miller looked to his fellow soldier, who was leaning against the wall at the opening of the hallway. He was glad to see Wentworth standing on his own two feet again, but the grim anxiety and absolute confusion that besieged Miller was too much to allow him to even force a smile.

"There's a lot of them like that, Doc," Wentworth said with almost no emotion in his voice. "Ours, tangos, civilians, women, children, even the fucking animals are coming back like that. Those things don't choose a side either. All political and national affiliations are fuck all for them now. The all have the same mission now, to kill anything with a pulse."

"You're certain he's dead?" Miller asked, looking back toward the mangled husk standing just on the other side of the door.

Wentworth looked his eyes directly into Miller's. "You're the medic, what do you think?" he answered.

Miller dropped his head and closed his eyes. "Fuuuuck", he whispered solemnly, resetting the door latches to the locked position. "How is this even possible?" he asked, returning his glassy gaze to Wentworth.

Wentworth dropped his eyes to the floor, trying to find the words to answer Miller. "Man, I don't know. We were in a firefight with terrorists just an hour ago. I understand war, but I have no fucking clue what this is." His eyes returned to Miller's. "On the way here, they were all over the road. Some more fucked up than others. Some were shot to hell, don't know if it was from an earlier fight, or if they were shot up after they turned. Others were just all chewed up and torn apart. My knowledge of what the fuck is going on is entirely based on what I've seen in the last hour. At this point, your guess is as good as mine."

Suddenly the two soldiers heard a loud bustle come from the other side of the door. They both jumped at the sound, each one wide eyed. Miller peered through the gap hoping to see a living soldier, or any sign of help. He sighed with disappointment.

"It's just two more of them tripping over junk," Miller announced with obvious dismay. Although he had accepted that what he was seeing was indeed reality, he could not begin to understand how it was even possible. Miller stared blankly out the small porthole, watching the three zombies stagger back and forth aimlessly.

"We need to secure this place as best we can," Wentworth ordered. "There's no telling how long we are going to be here or how many of them are outside."

The two soldiers sat in in the glowing candle light. Before returning to the area on the floor they had made their domain, they went from room to room, making sure there was no way in. They found a few partially expended AK magazines in various rooms. There was blood spattered across one of the walls and drops across the floor, leading from that room and going all the way to the main door. They didn't find anything useful to their situation, and all they had to defend themselves with were some broken furniture legs they could use as clubs, their M9s, and a M4 with only 16 rounds remaining in the magazine. Their hold was very secure, but if the need for them to fight ever arose, their situation would be dire.

Now they had been sitting in the hallway in the candlelight for what seemed like hours. Not much was happening outside from what they could hear. They would hear an occasional thump against various windows in the midst of the never ending howling and grunts of the dead that surrounded their fortification. Wentworth passed the time massaging his injured arm, as Miller laid on his back, staring up the flickering light, dancing across the high ceiling. Neither one of them has said a word in quite some time.

"It started out as a gunfight," Wentworth said, finally breaking the empty silence between them. "We got word that a bomb making factory was in the basement of a masque right down the street from the police station, and that it was heavily defended."

"Yeah, I remember all that," Miller interrupted. "We drove up and they started shooting RPKs and shit from the rooftop. Tell me what happened to the platoon."

"Well," Wentworth continued, "we were hitting them hard from positions all around their complex, but after a minute we realized Hadji wasn't shooting back at us. Whoever they were engaging was already inside with them. Realizing this, Lt. Spencer called us to cease fire so we wouldn't risk hitting any friendlies that may have been inside. He jumped on the radio to figure out who else was attacking the masque, and why we weren't informed of their presence, but that's when shit got crazy. We started hearing gun fire and screaming from other buildings around us. After a few seconds of that, it was coming from every direction, echoing from as far as we could hear. Gunfire, explosions. Pretty soon there were pillars of smoke over the rooftops in every direction, and all shit had happened within minutes. It sounded like the whole fucking city was at war with itself. Then this Hadji civilian ran from a shop behind our position. He was covered in blood and holding an AK. We yelled at him to drop his weapon, but he wasn't even looking at us. He was pointing the gun in the other direction, back toward the shop. Then a woman just burst from the door, also covered in blood. Man, she had at least four or five holes in her chest, but she was standing up, looking right at the guy. What fucked me up is that their expressions were all wrong."

"What do you mean by that?" Miller interrupted.

Wentworth blinked rapidly a few times, as if he was still trying to comprehend it himself. "The dude holding the AK, well his face was full of fear. And the woman who was all shot up, her face was full of rage," Wentworth answered as he stared into the dark hallway.

Miller blinked a few times himself.

"I'm not kidding, man," Wentworth went on, "that bitch was showing teeth and growling, like a fucking wolf. Then the guy with the AK literally started pissing himself, right there in front of us all. Once he starting muttering one of those Hadji prayers, I knew shit was no doubt about to get way more fucked up. Whatever was going on, he knew more about it than we did, and he was terrified, man."

Wentworth paused and looked at Miller for a moment, expecting him to say something along the lines of, "I don't understand." However, Miller didn't need to say a word, the shock was written all over his face.

"Anyway," Wentworth continued, "she lunged at him from twenty feet, but was on him in the blink of an eye. He got in a few shots before she took him down. He hit her at least twice I think, but it didn't faze her one bit. She took him to the ground and ripped a huge chuck of flesh from his neck with her teeth. Spencer yelled for her to stop, but she kept on tearing into the poor bastard and he kept on screaming. I don't know who it was, but someone in our squad took a shot at her while she was tearing the guy apart. The round hit her square in the chest, and once again, she gave zero fucks. We all started screaming for her to stop and get on the ground. That's when she acknowledged us for the first time."

Wentworth suddenly paused, his eyes wide open, still staring into space. He swallowed hard and continued speaking, wearing an almost blank expression, "Man, I've never seen so much hate.

I looked right into her eyes, and she looked right back into mine. I saw hell itself in that woman. She was no longer human, and I wasn't the only one who could see it. Five of us opened up into her, and she actually managed to get to her feet regardless. Her fucking arm flew off and we put a grouping into that's bitches chest so tight I could see through it. Then Lee starting working her with the SAW. The bitch's guts were spilling out everywhere, but she pushed toward us anyway. Her eyes, man, I've never seen anything like it."

Wentworth paused, pale as a ghost and frozen with an expression of wonderment. Several seconds passed and the man hadn't even blinked.

"Did we take her down?" Miller asked with a low tone, obviously distraught over what he was hearing.

"No," Wentworth answered blankly. "Lee literally cut her in half with the SAW. We stopped shooting because we figured she was spent. I shit you not, brother, that bitch starting using her good arm to drag herself toward us. And as if that wasn't fucked up enough, the guy she mangled right in from of us, well, he got up. Same damn chaos in his eyes. He wasn't looking at her though, he was staring right at us. Staring like he wanted to kill us the same way she killed him."

Miller's head was spinning at the words he was hearing. He didn't want to believe what he was hearing, it sounded absolutely crazy. Yet, he could picture it all in his head clearly as Wentworth went on. So clearly, as if Wentworth was narrating a movie Miller was watching in his mind. Despite the events that defied all conceived reality, Miller believed Wentworth. He not only believed him, he realized the scenes of events playing in his mind weren't just images, they were memories.

"What happened to the platoon?" Miller asked once again, quietly.

Wentworth's eyes began to water as the events played back in his mind. His voice thick with grief as he cleared his throat several times.

"Well," he began slowly, "I think the sound of the gunfire attracted the ones near us. I mean there was gunfire coming from every direction, but I know the SAW combined with the bursts from our carbines must have rang out particularly loud. The fucking things started pouring in from every direction. They were coming from every alley and doorway. We were surrounded by hundreds within minutes. Spencer organized us into a defensive echelon, and we were able to hold the line for a little bit, but they don't react to bullets at all. No fear, no hesitation, no pain. They just kept pushing forward. Lee started aiming at their legs with the SAW and chopped down an entire flank. Hell, making them trip and fall over one another seemed to be more effective than hitting them center mass. That still only slowed their advance. Plus they gained even more ground every time we had to reload. Eventually they broke our lines and started chewing us up.

Everyone started falling back to the center of the formation, trying to get into the Humvees, but they had cut us off. The guys on the turrets were doing their best to clear us a path, but it was no use. After a few minutes, the Humvees started driving forward. I don't know if they figured we were all fucked, or if they thought they could clear us a path by driving through them. It didn't matter either way. We were fighting them from every direction, within meters. There was no way we could keep up. Before I even realized it, the Humvees were gone."

Wentworth, smiled and reached out with his right arm slapping Miller on his chest. "That's when you had the bright yet obvious idea to use the 203 to blow a hole through the alley wall to our rear."

Miller looked at Wentworth as if he was waiting for him to continue a fragmented sentence. "Well, how many of us got through?"

Wentworth's expression returned a frown and he dropped his yes. "It was me, you, Lee, Johannson, Jackson, and a few others. We made it a few blocks before running into another hoard. That's when I boosted the truck and Johannson knocked you out. By the time I was able to drive away, the others were all dead. "

Miller just continued to stare up at the ceiling. Several more minutes went by, both soldiers taking up silence again.

Miller's mind was busy trying to comprehend the reality of what was going on. According to everything know to science, this was supposed to be impossible. Mankind had never taken seriously the chance that this very extinction level event may one day be reality. The mere notion of the dead walking the earth, consuming the living, had never been anything more than a concept explored by Hollywood for the sake of entertainment. Movies, television shows, videos games, even comic books. That's as seriously as any of this was ever taken. But now, out of nowhere and without explanation, it was a reality. How was this even possible?

"What do you think might have caused this?" Miller asked, finally breaking the silence.

Wentworth continued massaging his arm as though he had forgotten about the terrifying new threat that lurked just outside the bunker walls. "Don't know," he responded. "But I'm pretty sure some scientist back home is on the verge of cracking the mystery."

"You think this is going on back home?" Miller asked with an obvious underscore of panic in his voice. Until that moment, it had not occurred to Miller that the dead may be walking around in more than just the province they were in.

"I didn't say that, Doc," Wentworth replied, his annoyance obvious in his voice. "I'm just saying that it's highly likely the CDC Brainiac's back home are already figuring out a way to contain this shit. This shit is going to be just like the Ebola scare a few years back. It'll have everyone thinking it's the end of civilization as we know it, but by next week it'll all be over and forgotten by pretty much the entire world. Everyone will be tuning in to MTV to see which rich black man the Kardashians are going to ruin next."

Wentworth said this with ease, as if he was actually convinced. This actually made Miller feel a bit at ease despite the ridiculousness of Wentworth's hypothesis.

"I sure hope you're right", Miller chuckled. "Fuck those Kardashian bitches."

The two began to laugh, but their moment of light heartedness was interrupted by the thunderous boom of a nearby explosion.

"Shit!" Wentworth burred out, his eyes wide as softballs. That blast came from right outside! Take the M4 and make sure the door is still secured," Wentworth barked as he pointed to his M4 carbine. "There are 16 rounds left in the mag with one in the chamber. Do not shoot unless the door has been compromised and you have to push them back!"

Miller slung the M4 around his neck and released the magazine as he hurried toward the door. He had no idea what to expect. This made him nervous. It made him downright afraid. Miller had not only made it through Ranger School, but he survived four tours of combat in three countries. With each deployment, the enemies he faced were better trained, better equipped, and more radical than the last. Their networks were larger too. But this, this was totally different. Not even nine months of Ranger School and four combat deployments had prepared him to face this newest enemy he still could not fully grasp. He had no idea what tactics would work effectively against them, or if his weapons would even have an effect. Miller was downright terrified as he raced toward the door, reconciling to himself that his only hope of survival would be to learn a whole lot about this new undead enemy in a short amount of time.

Miller raised the rifle to his shoulder, pointing it toward the door as it came into view. He approached it cautiously, then sighed with relief to see it was unscathed. "It's good, the door is good to go!" He shouted down the hall toward Wentworth. He was waiting for a response from his fellow soldier but his attention was yanked back to the front of the building when three consecutive bangs rang out above his own voice.

"Shots fired!" Miller shouted. He could tell right away that whoever was shooting was not shooting at the door. The rounds were aimed in the opposite direction. All this commotion only seemed to excite the zombies, and their howls and shrieks rose to an ear piercing volume.

Miller raced to the door and peered through the porthole. He didn't see any fire, but there was a thick cloud of dust and smoke clouding the air. Then suddenly, he saw a soldier being illuminated by the quick flashes of the handgun he was discharging into the faces of the flesh eating corpses that were quickly surrounding him.

Miller's eyes widened at the number of zombies just outside the main entrance. There were dozens. Just moments before there was only a handful.

"Well, what the fuck!? Over!" Wentworth's voice rang from the hallway.

"It's a soldier, he's fighting them off!" Miller called. "I gotta get him in here!" Miller began unlatching the heavy locks that secured the door.

Miller moved with great haste, determined to get to the soldier before it was too late. Two more shots rang out, and Miller looked up in time to see the soldier look over his shoulder toward the bunker's main door. He must have heard Miller slamming the latches back as he unlocked the door.

Miller finally burst the door open and called to the soldier who was diligently fighting for his life. "In here soldier, come to me!"

Without hesitation, the soldier peeled away from his attackers and ran toward Miller, giving him just enough space to fire a short burst of rounds into the pursuing crowd of zombies.

As soon as the soldier was through the door, they both turned and slammed the entrance shut. Miller began resetting the latches as the tall soldier jammed his shoulder into it. The soldier was quite tall, and very strong looking. The mass of his muscular shoulders, arms, and thighs could be easily seen through his uniform.

"Well, shit on my chest and call me your sister. I was certain your candy ass was deader than Abe Lincoln by now!" Miller's new guest said in a raspy voice as the finishing touches were applied to securing the door.

"Lt. Spencer!" he shouted. "You're alive, man!"

The soldier looked back at him, acknowledging Miller's joy with a stiff grin. "You're God damn right brother," the soldier replied with smug confidence. "Can't no man kill Mad Max, living or dead. Fuck em' both, hooah."

"Hooah," replied Miller, a great feeling of confidence surging through him.

Lt. Madox "Mad Max" Spencer was the epitome of an Army Ranger. He was hard as nails, but had the respect and admiration of every Ranger in the regiment. Mad Max, as his Rangers affectionately referred to him, had a close relationship with his men, and he was without a doubt their favorite officer. Unlike the never ending pool of West Point grads that seemed to infest the Ranger brotherhood anymore, Lt. Spencer had history with the 75th Ranger Regiment before joining their ranks as an officer. He joined the army when he was 17, with the singular goal of following in his father's footsteps of becoming a Ranger of the 75th. It was his lifelong goal to join the ranks of the men who had raised him. He went through selection and passed Ranger school number one in his class. Naturally, he was the 75th's first pick after graduation. Now, just four years later, Spencer was the leader of First Platoon, with four squads under his command.

It wasn't the fact that Spencer joined the Rangers as an enlistee that won the respect of his men, it was the reason why. Spencer had deployed to Syria twice to combat the spread of ISIS during their peak, just after the Russian backed Syrian government had finally been over thrown. Bloodshed was at an all-time high all across the Middle East, and the wrong rebels had succeeded in over throwing Syria. Spencer's battalion had deployed there with the mission of taking critical facilities from ISIS, and disrupting their supply line. Within those two tours, Spencer had witnessed many injuries and deaths of his fellow rangers, many of which he was convinced were the result of incompetent leadership.

Spencer, like many of his fellow Rangers, was given the impression by most of the junior officers that they were only interested in their legacy. They wanted to win medals and make a name for themselves. In their selfish arrogance, they had made many poor decisions that lead to the injuries and deaths of several of Spencer's brothers.

Spencer dedicated himself to becoming an officer as he felt he could do a much better job at keeping his men alive, and seeing to it they had everything they needed to stay that way. Within three years, Spencer earned a college degree and his commission as an officer. To top it off, he stayed with the Rangers the entire time he worked to get his commission, including another deployment. He became an officer out of love for his men, and his men loved him back for it.

This was Spencer's fourth combat deployment as a Ranger, and his first as an officer. They were nearing the end of their deployment without suffering a single combat related injury under his command. But this had completely blindsided them all. None of the training or battles they had taken on in the past had prepared them to fight this new enemy, and in an instant, Spencer's entire platoon had been wiped out. Being a very strong minded man, Spencer finally found himself at a loss. Feeling overwhelmed and even a bit hopeless.

However, he had just found a few of his Rangers still alive, and fighting to survive. He wasn't going to let them down. Mad Max Spencer made up his mind right then and there that we was not going to lose any more Rangers today.

"What's the situation Ranger?" Spencer asked firmly, his eyes like stone looking at Miller's.

"Wentworth and I have been holed up in here about two hours. You're the first person we've seen since we arrived. Don't know if it's damaged, but we haven't been able to raise anyone on the horn."

"I've got a frag, three mags for my rifle, and two for my secondary. Do you have adequate arms, Doc?" the large soldier asked as paying no attention to the subtle fear in Miller's voice.

"No, Sir," Miller answered with a bit more tact, "We've got our side arms and 16 rounds in a carbine. The rest of our ammunition was expended while we were falling back."

Suddenly Wentworth interjected as he walked in from the hallway, "There is an RPK in the bed of the Haji truck we drove here in. I couldn't bring it inside. Miller was knocked out and I was shot in the arm, I couldn't bring it and him at the same time."

Spencer nodded his head at Wentworth in approval, "Well you made the right choice, Ranger. How's your arm?"

"Can't use it much, sir, but Miller did a good job at patching it up once he came to," he answered. "We also found a few AK mags in here, with a total of sixty-seven rounds which we consolidated into four mags. If we get a chance to make it to the RPK, we've got ammo."

Spencer took a deep breath and nodded again, he was impressed by the resilience of his men. Especially considering they were both only Pfcs with less than two years in the army. This was their first deployment, and they were keeping it together rather well, considering their current situation.

"This place secure?" Spencer asked as he peered through the port hole.

"Yes, sir", they both answered.

"Good shit", the iron jawed officer said, returning his gaze to his men. "Doc, you stand watch here. There were a whole shit ton of those things fast on my trail, they'll be here momentarily. Wentworth, give the nickel tour."

"Hooah," they both replied.

Suddenly, Miller's mind returned to the event that alerted them both to their Lieutenant's presence in the first place. "Sir," he blurted, "what was that explosion?"

"It was a pressure plate. One of the fuckers chasing me stepped on it. The blast blew me forward a few feet, but it took out a few corpses right behind me. Better those fuckers than me," he said with that smug grin on his face.

"You want me to look you over, sir?" Miller asked as his eyes danced all over Spencer with concern.

"Hell, I'm good to go. Just had the Ranger the fuck up and put boot to ass, that's all," Spencer said, his grin growing wider.

With that, the two soldiers exited the room, leaving Miller to survey the situation on the other side of the door.

As Spencer and Wentworth walked the empty halls of the complex, going room to room, he realized exactly how much of a tight space they were in. There was no sign of food, no running water, and no electricity, and only one way in and out. On top of that, there were a few dozen zombies just on the other side of their single entrance, with slew of several dozen more on their way. Spencer was certain the noise of the explosion and gunfire attracted the attention of every zombie within a mile.

He began to consider their options, neither of them any good. They could stay locked in the bunker, which was very secure. However without any food or water, they would eventually be forced into a desperate attempt to flee. There could possibly be a crowd of hundreds of those things waiting for them outside by then. Their other option was to make a run for it now. Fight their way to the truck and rap the RPK. Perhaps they could start it up and at least get a few hundred feet up the road. The problem with that was they didn't know which directions the zombies were coming in from, there was no guarantee there weren't more coming from the city north of them as were the ones that pursued them from the south. Plus, they'd be exposed until they could find more shelter, and there was no way of knowing where reliable shelter may be. They could try to make it to the mountains to the west, but one of them suffered a gunshot wound and another suffered a concussion. Either one of them could pass out or go into shock at any moment.

No matter what, their chances of survival were not very good. The platoon leader didn't see any light at the end of the tunnel for his men. He stared into space, deep in though.

Suddenly, the guns and moans of the zombies outside suddenly escalated into wailing and shrieks. Something had excited them.

"Oh shit," Miller's voiced echoed from the other end of the long hallway. "Shit, RPG!!"

There was a sudden, deafening thunder that rang out through the halls of the bunker. The dust clinging to the concrete surfaces of the bunker was knocked into the air, filling the hallways and rooms with thick, gray clouds of dust.

"Miller!!" Spencer yelled out, pressing his hands to this throbbing temples. "Doc! Doc, are you with me!?"

The large Ranger grabbed his subordinate and pulled him to his feet, and down the hallway toward the last known position of their friend. "Miller!" he continued to call.

As they approached the end of the hallway, nearing the front door, the dust cloud grew even thicker, reducing visibility to only a few feet. There was also a sudden increase in temperature, the air becoming very hot.

Just as Spencer was about to call for Miller again, the soldier staggered through the thick dust cloud and into view. Blood was flowing from his ears and his eyes were squeezed shut. His nose and cheeks were singed from the heat of the blast. Choking on the thick airborne dust, he blindly reached with both hands toward his friends. "I'm hit!" he yelled, unaware that his fellow soldiers were just feet in front of him.

"Jesus, Doc!" Wentworth gasped as he embraced Miller with both arms. "You're okay, Miller! You're alright!"

Suddenly the painful, terrified screams of several men, shouting in Arabic, filled the hallways.

"Stay here and don't move until I tell you", Spencer ordered, then running toward the twisted metal that used to be the main entrance door.

No sooner had Spencer disappeared through the mangled door did the sound of gun fire erupt through the wall.

"I'm engaging tangos," Spencer yelled during a split second break in the chaos." Then the gunfire continued.

Wentworth examined Miller as he leaned him against the wall. Miller was in bad shape, but he was still in once piece.

He reassured Miller that he was going to be okay, and that he had only gotten the wind knocked out of him as the exchange of M4 and AK gunfire continued. The thumping sound of M203 firing a 40mm grenade was followed by another explosion just moments later. After a few more seconds, the only thing that could be heard was a man shouting in Arabic, terror consuming his cries. Then painful shrieks, which were immediately muffled by the excited howls of the dead.

Spencer's voice suddenly bellowed through the hall, "Get your weapon and fall in on me, move your asses now.

Wentworth's pulse was pounding through his plate carrier. He could feel his pulse in his neck. He unslung the rifle hanging from Miller's neck and swung it around his own. Miller's eyes were now halfway open, and looking directly into his own. "Time to go, buddy!" he shouted. He knew Miller couldn't hear him, but it was important Miller understood what was about to happen.

With a nod, Miller grasped the back straps of Wentworth's body armor and followed him down the hall. Within seconds they arrived at the entrance to see the warped and punctured remains of the front door. Clearly Miller jumped to the side before impact, that's the only explanation for him still being in one piece.

Wentworth looked to see Lt. Spencer standing in the open, just ten feet from the opening, pointing his weapon into a crowd of rapidly approaching zombies. For the moment, they were distracted by the bodies of several ISIS fighters, which they were consuming. 50 yards beyond them, the burning wreckage of a large truck illuminated the night sky. Spencer must have taken it out when he fired the 203 mounted to his M4.

"Rangers," Spencer yelled over his shoulder, snapping Wentworth into the fight, "Follow me!!"

He then ran forward into the crowd, taking shots at the zombies that were closest to him. Shooting quick bursts into their faces, one by one. Wentworth followed after him shouldering his rifle as best as he could. He could feel Miller's toes banging into his boot heels, but he was determined to make it through the path his ferocious platoon leader was carving for them.

Wentworth had never been this close to the dead before. The dead reached out to him as they passed through. He could feel their fingertips scrape across his arms as they reached out to grab him and yank him in. Many had pale, yellow eyes. Their shirts were plastered with saliva and blood that ran from their mouths. He could feel their stale breath, thick with the smell of death as they howled with excitement, their eyes mad with an unquenchable thirst for warm blood.

They were half way through the crowd when Wentworth realized Spencer was leading them toward the white truck he and Miller arrived here in. Perhaps they would try to make one more getaway in the expended vehicle. Finally, they were through the crowd.

"Get in that truck and fire it up!" Spencer roared. The large Ranger turned around to provide cover for his two soldiers as they staggered passed him. Wentworth flung the door open and jumped into the driver seat as Miller clung to the side of the truck. "Fuck! Wentworth yelled with angry frustration. "It won't start, sir! This thing is fucked!"

Hearing this, Spencer ran to the bed of the truck, preparing to grab the RPK Wentworth alerted him to earlier. "It's gone!" he shouted banging both his hands against the truck bed. Those fuckhead Haji's must have grabbed it. They were shooting at me with it from the back of the truck I blew up."

Miller, standing with his back leaning against the vehicles, drew his sidearm and pointed it into the crowd of approaching zombies. The other two distracted Rangers didn't realize the hoard had closed to within just 20 feet of them.

"Aahh, aaahhhhh!" Miller screamed frightfully, altering his friends to the ever closing danger.

Spencer spun around and fired a burst into the approaching hoard. "Fuck it, we gotta move!" he shouted at Wentworth.

The three men ran to the other side of the truck, taking shelter as Spencer grabbed his only remaining grenade.

"Frag out!" he shouted as he threw it into the front of the crowd. The grenade went off and the shrapnel clattered loudly into the other side of the truck they were using as a barrier. Several dozen zombies were taken down by the blast, with others toward the rear staggering and tripping over the one that had fallen in front of them. This was their opportunity.

"Go, go, go!" Spencer yelled pointing toward an open field behind them. There was nowhere else to go. Their shelter had been compromised, and there were no lights in the distance to indicate the existence of the nearby city. Only the howls of the dead could be heard in the empty darkness of the night.

The three soldiers ran into a nearby field, their figures masked by darkness. The sounds of the wailing began to lessen slightly, and the men slowed their pace to a cautious jog.

"I don't think they see us," Wentworth whispered. His eyes darting wildly through the dark.

He was right. The silhouettes of the dead could barely be seen all around them, but they were scattered for the most part, none heading in any single direction, or toward them.

"Okay, let's just lay low and regroup," Spencer whispered, "let's count ammo and try to get some idea of what direction we should go."

The three had found an impact crater, most likely formed by the detonation of an IED, and hunkered down into it. They consolidated their remaining ammo between four rifle mags, and one loaded mag in each handgun. Miller's condition had improved. He still couldn't hear very well, but at least his vision had returned for the most part. He was still a bit disoriented, but he was coherent and walked on his own.

Spencer was debating if it would be safer for them to move at night, with hopes of reaching the foothills a few miles west of their current position. Moving at day would give them better visibility, but it would provide the same for the dead.

"Listen up," Spencer whispered, placing both his hands on Wentworth's shoulders. We gotta make a break for the high ground while we can. Its best we move now while those fuckers can't track us. Hooah?"

"Hooah, sir", Wentworth answered. "I'm going to take a piss before we get moving."

To that, Spencer replied, "don't go far, and don't shake more than twice."

Wentworth chucked under his breath and cautiously stepped from the hole. He took a few steps and began to urinate, cautiously checking over both shoulders for any approaching zombies. Wentworth finished up and turned around to rejoin his friends in the crater.

BAAAAMMMMMMM!!!!!! A bright flash lit up the night's sky in an instant, then everything was dark again. Rubble rained down on Spencer as he covered Miller with his own body.

"Sniper!" Wentworth called from the darkness. "Contact, sniper!!"

Spencer rolled Miller to his back, making sure the soldier could see his face with the tiny bit of illumination emanating from the star lit night sky. "Stay here. Do you understand me? Stay here," Spencer ordered Miller, who nodded his head quickly to show he understood what he was to do.

Spencer then stood up and jolted from the concealment of the crater to the last spot he had seen Wentworth. A huge dust cloud masked Wentworth completely.

"Sniper, take cover," Wentworth's voice range out from the cloud.

Spencer entered the haze, his eyes carefully scanning the ground for his friend. Then he saw him, laying on his back, looking in the direction of the bunker they had fled, pointing a mangled hand in the direction of truck still burning brightly in the distance.

"Take it easy Wentworth, you gotta keep it down", Spencer said as he reached into his IFAK and pulled out a tourniquet.

"One of them is still alive," Wentworth continued, clearly disoriented from the blast. "He fucking shot me, I think he got me in the hand."

"There's no sniper," Spencer replied, "you stepped on a mine".

Wentworth looked astonished by what his platoon leader said. He looked down elevated both legs slightly off the ground, to see that his left leg was bleeding badly and his right leg was missing below the knee.

"Oh fuck! Ohhhh, God, oh fuck!" he wailed.

Spencer pressed a hand to the flailing soldier's mouth, "Shhhh, man you gotta be quiet. Those things are all around us. They heard the blast and they're looking for us. You gotta keep it together man, focus."

Wentworth laid there, doing his best to process what his platoon leader was telling him as he took in the damage he had suffered.

"I gotta apply this tourniquet," Spencer blurted. "Look away take a deep breath. You gotta take the pain, man. Hold it in."

Wentworth looked away and shut his eyes, then Spencer went to work applying the tourniquet to what remained of Wentworth's leg. The injured soldier groaned in pain, biting down hard on his own hand as he held the other one.

Spencer knew the situation was grave. He could hear the moans and howls of the dead approaching from all directions. It would only be a matter of time before they would be on top of them. Spencer drew the handgun from the holster on Wentworth's right thigh. He took it off safe and placed it in his good hand. "Don't fire until I tell you," he ordered.

"Roger," he whispered through the pain.

Spencer looked back to the crater to see Miller standing on his feet, holding the M4, his face full of grief as he looked down upon his critical injured friend. The same friend that worked so hard to save his life.

The sound of howling zombies grew nearer and nearer, but above that, there rose another. It sounded faintly like a distant buzz saw. As the sound became louder, Spencer realized it was a helicopter. A small one, most likely some kind of light scout helicopter.

His eyes grew wide and he looked down to see the same expression across Wentworth's face.

Just then, the sound of gunfire rang out from just feet away. The two looked up to see Miller shooting out of the crater. The muzzle flash from each shot briefly illuminated the figures of zombies, approaching only meters away.

Spencer grabbed his rifle and engaged the zombies nearest to Miller. He carefully shot at them, one at a time. The noise of the helicopters rotors beating the air grew louder as it approached.

Wentworth holstered his pistol and fumbled through his hip kit, franticly searching for something we obviously thought would turn the tables.

The noise from the helicopter was louder, within a few hundred yards, but they couldn't see it as they were busy engaging the zombies that were almost within arm's reach. Suddenly, Spencer saw something red flashing wildly from his peripheral vision. He looked down to see Wentworth holding a red flashlight, waving it wildly in effort of getting the helicopter's attentions.

Suddenly green and red lights flashed in the sky just a few meters from them and the helicopter did a low pass. It was an MD530. Spencer knew right away the only unit in the area operating those helicopters was a PMC hired by the American government to provide transport and security to UN diplomats in country.

The helicopter made another low pass, flaring a bit in order to slow its airspeed. It came to a hover, just ten feet off the ground, kicking up sand with the powerful downwash from its five rotor blades.

"We're out of here!" Spencer yelled to Wentworth. "I'll be right back!" Spencer ran to the crater, and slapped Miller on the shoulder. "Let's go!" he barked. He then slung his rifle behind his back and reach down to lift Wentworth into a fireman carry over his shoulders.

Wentworth let out a painful scream as Spencer lifted him over his large shoulders. They broke into a solid stride toward the helicopter which was hovering just 50 meters away. The helicopter remained hovering in order to stay out of danger presented by the dead, but it touched down once the men had made it half way.

Miller was to the rear, still a bit disoriented and struggling to keep us with his hyper athletic platoon leader. He could see the dust from the helicopter just a ways in front him. Suddenly a thunderous crack accompanied by a bright yellow flash knocked him to his back. A wave of heat rushed over Miller, stinging his eyes and drying them out badly.

He looked down to examine himself, and saw pieces of metal protruding from his chest and stomach. They cut into his flack vest, so he had no way of knowing how deeply they had penetrated. Another had pierced his thigh, causing a steady stream of blood to run. Realizing he wasn't the one who detonated what he believed was a pressure plate, he looked in the direction of the helicopter. He saw Spencer and Wentworth, both laying on the ground, neither one moving. It was too dark for him to see them clearly but he could tell by the way the dust and debris was raining down heavily on them, that Spencer had detonated the device.

He saw another silhouette approaching from the direction of the helicopter. The figure dropped to its knees near the men, as if examining them. The figure then stood up and looked toward the helicopter, waving its hand quickly in front of its neck. Then the figure looked toward Miller and quickly approached him. As the person came into view, Miller was able to see the figure more clearly. It was a man wearing a dark jacket top and khaki pants. He was wearing a helicopter crew helmet with AN PVS15 night vision goggles mounted to the forehead of the helmet. He had an M249 Para slung from his neck, resting against a dark plate carrier. The operator took a knee right next to Miller and flashed a small light into his eyes. After taking his pulse, the operator stood up, waving his hands toward the helicopter. Within seconds, another similar looking crew member arrived and knelt down to Miller's other side. They hoisted the man from the ground and carried him to the small helicopter. They laid him on the floor along the bottom of a single row of seats. The airman placed a headset with a microphone over Miller's ears, which would protect his hearing from the deafening wail of the turboshaft engine and allow the crew to communicate with him.

Miller looked up at the ceiling of the helicopter, feeling himself lifting up. Bright yellow flashes from the crew member's gun danced across the ceiling as they took to the night sky. The air man ceased firing once they were out of the zombies reach. Miller rolled his head around and could see the light of the burning truck illuminating a massive hoard of zombies. They were gathering around its light, like moths drawn to flames.

Once it was out of sight, Miller looked up into the night sky. He had no idea what would come next, but he was determined to meet it head on.

"Hey, Ranger", the crew member's voice crackled through the headset. For the first time in what seemed like forever, Miller could actually make out what was being said to him. "You're one hard mother fucker! You're going to make it!" the airman continued, grasping Miller's hand with his own.

"Hooah," Miller grunted into the mic, a slight, smug grin settling on his face.

STORY SEVEN

THE TOWN

"Yo, Rookie...looks like you caught your first real assignment," Rick said as he threw a case file on Maria's desk.

"Finally!" Maria said, excitement in her voice. It had been six months since she had left Quantico and she was dying to get a case. Her career path was already mapped out in her mind and she was eager to get started.

"Don't look so excited, this is a case that no one else wanted," Rick said.

"I don't care what it is, a case is a case and I am going to nail it, you just watch and see," she said opening the file.

Rick watched as Maria's face changed from happiness to disgust. "Nice I know, apparently you have a serial killer on the loose in Ederfield, Ohio."

"Where the hell is that?" Maria asked.

"It's a really small town, population 2200 or less, not really on our radar, but it seems that every two years a serial killer surfaces and kills a string of locals in the most brutal of ways."

"From these pictures I can see what you mean, damn." Maria said. "This guy is a savage!"

"Well, he's all yours, nobody else wants to get stuck in the back country."

"Your flight is already booked, you leave tomorrow at 7," Rick said as he headed away.

Maria continued to peruse the file; there were loads and loads of pictures of victims, their bodies or what is left of them mutilated and distorted, some of them missing vital body parts, one was even headless. 'The Ederfield Mangler,' she thought to herself, that had a nice ring to it and she was going to catch him.

When she touched down in Ohio, it looked like any other state to her. It wasn't New York but it was actually quite nice, she headed to the rental car agency and picked up the car which was prepaid for by the bureau. She got inside and punched her destination into the GPS and she was on her way. The case file had Richard Spencer listed as the lead investigator on the case so she intended on speaking with him as soon as she arrived. Not even stopping for a bathroom break, she made her way to Ederfield as quickly as she could, she was excited and she wanted to delve right into it.

When she finally made it to Ederfield, after six hours of driving, she was exhausted, but not too exhausted that she didn't stop by the local police station to meet and speak to Richard.

"Hi, I am Maria Caffrey, I'm looking for Richard Spencer," she said as she entered the small police station that looked as though it was housed in an old church or something.

"And you are?" asked a tall, well-built man with a u-shaped scar over his left eye, his voice was husky and sounded really sensual. If Maria wasn't bent on the task at hand she might have noticed, but as it stood, she didn't.

"I just said that I am Maria Caffrey," she said, visibly annoyed.

"I heard you, but what do you want with Richard Spencer?" he asked.

"Look cut the bull, is he here or not I have urgent business with him," she said.

"I'm Richard Spencer and again, what do you want!" he said, beginning to share her annoyance.

"Good, I'm from the FBI and I am here to investigate the recent murders," she said.

"I thought they were sending a man, never thought they would send a little lady, none the less, I think you best run back home and leave well enough alone down here, what happens in this town doesn't concern you," he said turning away.

"Wh…what, didn't you hear me well, I am here to catch the son of a bitch that is slaughtering these folks," she shouted.

"Who said it was a son of a bitch," he said, not turning to look at her.

"What the hell do you mean?" she asked frustrated.

"I mean who ever said that it was a person killing these folks, you need to go back to wherever it is you came from," Richard said again.

"I'm not leaving until I get to the bottom of this and you can't scare me away either," she said.

"Well it's your funeral," he said, dropping a huge case file into her arms, "happy reading in the meantime."

"Where's the morgue?" she asked.

"Right down the street, we keep our deceased at the funeral home, so you will find whatever you are looking for there."

Maria lugged the file out through the door with her and dropped it in the passenger side of the car. She stood up and looked down the street, from where she was, she could see the funeral parlor, so she decided to walk there instead of driving.

When she opened the door, it chimed loudly, startling her. Before she was inside properly, an old man approached her, it seemed as though he appeared out of nowhere.

"May I help you Maria?" he asked.

"How do you know my name?" she asked, "did that pain in the butt Richard tell you that I was on my way?"

"You are here to see Professor Hernandez I suppose," he said, not answering her.

"Yes I am," she said slowly, being inside of the parlor was making her feel weird and the strange funeral director wasn't helping.

"I didn't get your name," she said, trying to add a bit of normalcy to the eerie exchange.

"I never gave it," he said as he motioned for her to follow him.

If she thought that the front part of the funeral parlor was strange, there were no words for how she felt when she was inside of the morgue area. The entire room was spotless and it smelled of bleach, which was all fine, it was the mounted animal heads that seemed terribly out of place and definitely in bad taste.

The funeral director pulled out the body, what she saw was even worse than the pictures; it looked as though his body was riddled with holes from end to end. Chunks of his body were removed leaving only empty holes behind.

"What do you think could have done this?" she asked.

"I think you should leave," the funeral director said.

"Give me his personal effects, I want to take a look at them," she said, ignoring his warning.

He walked slowly across the room and handed her a clear bag which he took from a drawer. It contained the professor's wallet among other things.

"Thanks a lot," she said as she left the creepy parlor. As soon as she stepped out the door, there was a whizz of police cars, well two police cars to be exact. She jumped inside of her car and followed them, hoping to catch a lead of some kind. When they finally stopped, it was on the outside of a large white house; her face was as white as a sheet when she saw what had happened. There strung up on the house was an elderly man, he was naked and the same holes were throughout his body, his mouth was opened and he was strung up by his mouth and nostrils. He looked maimed, his privates barely hanging on, it looked like mince, as though it was chewed upon. The mere sight of him made her feel as though she wanted to puke, but she tried to hold it in. The fact that her name was also written across the front of the house in blood did not escape her either, in fact, for the first time she was feeling scared.

"Scared yet?" Richard turned and said to her. She didn't answer him.

"How could someone get so high to do that, that house is at least 22ft," she asked.

"You are asking the wrong questions, who said it was a someone?" he replied.

Feeling frustrated, Maria got into her car and drove to the bread and breakfast that she was to be staying at.

"Hello Maria," a pretty middle-aged woman greeted her as she walked in.

"How the hell do you know my name, you people are creepy as hell!" she exclaimed, tired and frustrated.

"Oh, I'm sorry, it is just that you are the only person who has to check in today, it isn't as though we have the most business," she replied.

"I'm sorry," Maria said, "I'm just a bit on edge."

The receptionist gave her the room key and escorted her to her room. It was nice enough, had plenty room for her to work, not that she was sure that she even wanted to. She was seriously thinking about going back home, there was something strange going on in this town and it seemed as though all the locals knew about it and they weren't too keen on letting her in on the secret.

Maria didn't know just how long the screaming had begun, when she finally heard it she jumped up from sleeping with a start. She listened for a bit more to make sure that she wasn't dreaming, when the screaming continued, she reached into her night stand and took out her gun. She ran downstairs, that is where it was coming from. For a moment she was frozen, she stood there with her gun in her hand, unable to fire, the receptionist was screaming wildly as a brown mass wrapped itself around her, forcing itself through her body until finally she stopped screaming, the life drained from her. Maria finally jolted into action and fired at the monster. It stopped for a moment, the noise of the shot gaining its attention. Pulling itself viciously from the receptionist who was now riddled with holes, it began to approach Maria. She kept on firing; it was only when she was out of bullets that she realized that they didn't wound it in the slightest.

"Maria," it said in a loud thunderous voice, "I have been waiting for you."

She started to run up the stairs, fear gripping her.

"You are afraid, I can feel it," the monster said.

In her fear, she jumped through the closed window, cutting her face and hands. She landed on her feet miraculously and sprinted towards the police station, never once looking back, never even caring that she was just wearing her underwear.

"What the hell is going on in this town?" she screamed as she burst through the door of the police station.

"What happened to you?" Richard asked.

"What happened to me is, I just saw a brown, I can't believe that I am saying this, but I saw a brown monster killing the receptionist at the hotel, then it tried to kill me" she said.

"What! Poor Kitty," Richard said and sent a patrol car over to the hotel, he then called the funeral parlor to let him know what had happened.

"It was horrible!" screamed Maria.

"Did you know about this?" she asked.

When he didn't respond, she knew that he did. "Why would you let something like that run free in your town," she asked hysterically.

"And just what do you propose we do about it?" he asked, "It's a monster, plus he only feeds every two years."

"You sound crazy," she said.

"You are the crazy one, he wants you from the looks of it and it isn't luck that you got away tonight, it wanted you, it wants to toy with you and sooner or later you will end up like Kitty if you don't leave this town."

"Do you know why it is here? Do you know anything at all about it?" she asked.

"I just told you what I know, in case you are wondering we aren't friends, it comes and it feeds and it leaves." He said.

"Get out while you can, you can stay here the night, not that here is any protection, but at least you won't be alone."

"Here's a blanket," he said, throwing it at her. She caught it and covered herself with it.

"Where are you going?" she asked when she realized that he was leaving.

"Home," he said coolly, "I have a house and a dog."

"So you're just going to leave me here?" she asked shocked.

"You are FBI, I am sure that you can take care of yourself, besides I have three deputies on duty." He said.

Maria looked around at the deputies; they looked old and decrepit, like the perfect offerings for the monster. It was then that it began to make sense to her; all of the victims were either middle aged or old. It was as though the monster was attacking only them. With the exception of her and like two more victims who were visiting, everyone was old.

If only she had her files, she would be able to piece it all together. At least she had access to the station's computers, that way she could do some research using their files. She asked one of the deputies to log her in and he readily obliged. She started by looking at all of the victims, just as she had thought they were all old or tourists and the murders started from years earlier, from what she could tell, they started from the time the town was founded. She looked at the professor's file, it seemed as though he wasn't always from Ederfield; he had come to live there only a few months before, she needed to get back to the hotel to take a look at his stuff. When she slipped out of the station, no one even knew.

Once she was back in her room, she started to dig through the professor's stuff. He had a black notebook that was filled with writing; it was haphazardly written which made it a bit difficult to understand, especially in the dim light. Policemen were still on the outside and she had to climb a tree round back to get inside. She didn't want to alert them of her presence. One name kept reappearing in the book over and over 'Richard Spencer,' Maria thought it to be strange, why would there be a connection between the monster and Richard. The professor obviously had a few screws loose. It was only when an old photo dropped out of the book that she realized that there really was a connection. It looked to be a really old picture of Richard, dated back to when the town was founded in 1798. A strange feeling washed over her, how could that be, probably it was a relative or something like that, but deep down inside she knew that it couldn't be, the man in the picture looked exactly like Richard, relatives couldn't share identical scars and the man in the picture had the same u-shaped scar which Richard has over his left eye. A chill went through her, if this really was a picture of him, that would make him well over two hundred years old, surely that was impossible, yet the evidence was staring her right in the face. The professors book had graphically drawn pictures of what she assumed was Richard and the monster, it looked as though he believed that they were one and the same, able to come apart whenever it was necessary; he referred to him as a 'soul sucker' taking the essence of others to maintain his own life and even to extend it. Maria couldn't believe what she was reading, it felt like something out of a horror movie, it just couldn't be true, only she had seen the monster with her own eyes.

Slipping back through the window, she began to jog back to the station; she wanted to be there in case Richard returned. The last thing she wanted him to know was that she suspected him. She needed to get home first, to feel safe again.

The attack was sudden, she felt a blow to her head; she felt hot blood streaming down her face. Dazed she looked around frantically to see who had struck her. "You couldn't leave well enough alone, could you, I really didn't want to do this but I have no choice," Richard said.

"Richard is that you? What are you talking about?" she asked, trying to sound clueless.

"Oh, don't bullshit me pretty lady, I have been around way too long to get fooled by the likes of you," he said.

"You read the professor's book and you saw me, I tried to get the picture and the stupid book from the parlor but I couldn't find where that old fool had them," he said.

"Please Richard, you don't have to do this," she begged.

"Oh, so you do know about me," he said laughing wickedly.

Maria watched as he began to separate, the brown mass pulling itself away from him, he was laughing all the while.

"Maria, Maria, Maria," the monster taunted, she began to run, but before she was able to even get anywhere, it was upon her. She could feel the weight of it, weighing heavily down on her body, trapping her on the ground, rendering her defenseless. Richard was still laughing, he sounded frenzied, as though he was enjoying what was happening to her. The monster slithered up and down her body as though it was looking for just the right spot to enter. Maria lay motionless, the fear of her impending death too much to bear. It entered her leg first, the pain was excruciating, she screamed at the top of her voice. The monster stuffed her mouth, stopping the sound from coming. She heard the bones in her leg break as it forced its way through, another tendon began to force its way through her other leg. Through the corner of her eye, she could see Richard, he looked as though he was harnessing her pain. She felt it go through her natural opening and burst out through her stomach, at his point the pain was just too much and she passed out. The monster continued to penetrate her body, leaving only holes where her breasts had been and where her eyes had been, when it was finished with her lifeless body, it returned to Richard. He glowed in the darkness, filled with all the life essence that he would need to last him another two years.